The Hoyden
And The Rake

The Hoyden
And The Rake

VICTORIA PRICE

DEDICATION

To all those who believe in true love.

CHAPTER ONE

Two cloaked figures furtively tiptoed down the stairs and through the hall. The back door opened with a slight squeak as they slipped outside. The two figures hurried toward the waiting carriage, which lost no time in speeding through the sleeping London city as the rosy fingers of dawn trailed its painted veil across the horizon.

Miss Fiona Cavendish let out the breath she had been holding in a long-drawn-out sigh as she pulled her cape closer in the dark carriage. She turned her bright eyes and wide smile to the other occupant of the carriage.

"We've done it, Marcie. Soon we will be in Scotland at my Uncle Henry's house, and there we will stay until Ted returns from the war."

Her maid and abigail, Marcie Hinckley, slumped and yawned. "Miss, what if your cousin finds out and tries to bring you back?"

"She has no way of knowing where we are bound, so she cannot very well find us, can she?"

"What about Mr. Harry? Won't he be angry?"

"I don't care much about Cousin Harry's anger. He is the reason I have had to flee my home."

"But miss, what if Master Ted were to come back . . . wouldn't he be worried?"

"Marcie, when my brother returns, then all my worries are over, and I will be the happiest girl in England. So, stop worrying and get some rest."

Marcie looked dubious. Smoothing the folds of her fur-lined pelisse, Fiona sighed and gazed out of the window as they left London behind on their way north. Her thoughts wandered to her brother. He was not dead, she knew that in her heart, but he must be hurt or taken prisoner, for otherwise, he would have written her. *Oh Lord, please let him come back to me,* she said the oft-repeated prayer in her mind. After having lost her parents at the tender age of fourteen, she couldn't bear to lose her only surviving family member.

Tears pricked her eyes as she remembered the happy times when her parents had still been alive. After their death, Cousin Sadie, Mama's cousin, had come to live with them with her son, Harry. The death of his parents had affected Ted deeply, and he had returned from university a changed man. He had taken residence at Red Oaks, his country estate. Cousin Sadie had seen fit to send Fiona to a finishing school for ladies, and she had only seen Ted during the holidays. By the time she had returned home for her debut into polite society, he had left to join the war effort. Despite seeing so little of him the last few years, the bond between brother and sister had only grown stronger, and they had corresponded with regularity until a few months ago when Ted's letters had abruptly ceased to arrive. It was true that the post was unpredictable and that it took months to reach her, but he had corresponded most regularly until then. Worse, none of the officers returning from the war could tell her any news about him. He was reported missing in action, but Fiona had not given up hope. *I would know if he were dead.* If only he would come back, she would not have to flee her own home. Sighing, Fiona closed her eyes wearily. The motion of the carriage made her drowsy, and she fell asleep.

She woke up with a start when the carriage stopped some hours later. Looking out the window, she saw a small hostelry, with a sign outside proclaiming it to be the Wandering Goose Inn. The hostlers were milling about, taking care of the horses. The sun was shining brightly overhead. A rumble in her stomach reminded her that they hadn't breakfasted. After rousing the sleeping Marcie, she made her way into the inn.

Soon they were ensconced in a private parlor and enjoying a simple lunch of bread and cheeses and piping hot tea. The food revived them and even set Marcie to start smiling. But their lunch was interrupted when a flurry of activity indicated that another carriage had pulled up behind her own.

Through her parlor window, Fiona watched with interest as a dark-haired man alighted and, after a word to one of the hostlers, made his way into the inn. His broad shoulders and height proclaimed him a Corinthian. His attire, which was of the best quality and rather somber, made him out to be a gentleman. As if aware of her appraisal, he turned and looked back at her. Dark eyes pierced her own, under an eyebrow that was raised in question. His mouth quirked in a cynical smile. He was not at all handsome but rather grim looking, she decided. Under the sharp onslaught of his eyes, her own wavered and dropped as heat painted her cheeks a vivid crimson. Her confusion was fortunately not noticed by Marcie, who had gone to tidy herself up. When she returned, the two ladies boarded their carriage and resumed their journey north.

"What is your plan, miss?" Marcie asked her mistress.

"As I have said, I just want to get to my uncle's estate in Scotland, Marcie," Fiona responded mechanically, her thoughts still on the stranger she had spied at the inn.

"How long should we stay there, miss?" Marcie persisted.

"Until I marry or Ted returns, whichever comes first."

"Miss, you have had eight offers so far. Did none of them suit?"

"Marcie, I will only marry a man whom I love and who loves me for my mind, not just my face and my wealth. And to date, my suitors have been either gold diggers, ancient, widowers, insipid bores, chauvinistic pigs, or, of course, Harry Albrighton!" Fiona said this last name with so much aspersion that Marcie burst into giggles.

"Master Harry was persistent, wasn't he, miss?"

"He was a pest! It's because of him and his mother, Cousin Sadie, that I have had to leave my own home. They have had the audacity not only to make themselves my guardians in Ted's absence but also to push Harry's interests on me! Now that is truly intolerable."

"But miss, what if Master Ted does not come before your birthday?"

"He will, Marcie, he must!" Fiona cried out loudly as if her voice could ensure her dear brother's return. If Ted were not to return by the time her birthday rolled around in a month, Fiona faced an impossible choice. Her maternal grandmother had left her a fortune that would allow her to be independent of Harry and Cousin Sadie, but the fortune was hers only if she married before her twenty-first birthday. If not, it reverted to Ted, and hence to Harry as Ted's heir. She would be penniless and at the mercy of Harry Albrighton. If Ted did not return before

3

her birthday, then Fiona would have to choose a husband and enter a loveless marriage. Her emotional response silenced Marcie, and Fiona settled back on the cushions and fell into a reverie. Her mind replayed the unpleasant scene with Harry that had prompted her impulsive departure from her beloved home.

<hr />

"Fiona, you must see the benefits that an alliance with me offers. I am Ted's heir, and as my wife, you can continue to live in your family home. We know each other well and so will suit just fine," Harry had wheedled until she had lost her temper.

"I cannot possibly marry you." Fiona's voice rose in frustration as she repeated the words for the fourth time. "I am determined that I will only marry for love or not at all."

The oily smile on Harry Albrighton's face diminished but did not disappear. "Fiona, my dear, I do love you, and you will come to love me if you would only give me the chance to prove to you that I am worthy of you."

"Do stand up, Harry. No matter! I will not marry until Ted returns."

Harry Albrighton did as she asked and moved to perch on the sofa next to her. "Fiona, I know this is difficult for you, but we must accept that Ted may never return."

His words induced unbidden tears in Fiona's eyes, and she cast them down. She saw that he planned to draw her into his arms so she may weep on his shoulder. She thwarted him by instead standing and moving to the window of the luxurious parlor. "Ted will return, and I will not hear otherwise."

"Fiona, if you will not see reason, as your guardian and the head of this household, I must act on your behalf. My dear cousin, you are now twenty and are of marriageable age, yet have turned down no fewer than eight offers, not including my own."

As if on cue, her cousin Sadie entered the parlor just then. Fiona suspected that she may have been listening at the door. She shook her head, trying to dismiss the uncharitable thought. However, she had cause to be upset with Cousin Sadie and Harry. It wasn't that Cousin Sadie was unkind, but she expected Fiona to fit the mold of the debutante: pretty,

4

girly, and with the sole aim in life of marrying the highest-ranking suitor.

Cousin Sadie was Papa's distant relative who had moved in to take care of Fiona and her brother, Ted, after their parents' demise. She and her son, Harry, had made their permanent home with them. Harry was a year younger than Ted and immensely admired him. The two of them had attended first Eton and then Cambridge together. Fiona's parents had died a few years ago in a carriage accident and left Fiona and Ted orphaned.

Though Harry had grown up with Ted and Fiona, they were so different that they never bonded. Harry had many annoying qualities that did not endear him to his cousins. They especially abhorred his whiny ways and the way he twisted the truth just to make himself look better to his mother. The orphaned siblings merely tolerated Harry for the sake of Cousin Sadie and usually gave him a wide berth. When Ted left on his war effort, Harry had inserted himself into Fiona's life and tried to control her activities. And he had recently been pressuring her to get married and coaxing his mother to aid him in this endeavor. Between the dour looks and barbed references to ungrateful chits from Cousin Sadie and the incessant pressure from Harry, life at home had become a nightmare.

He had assumed command of the household, controlling Ted's estate and, by extension, Fiona's freedom. Fiona would not come into her full inheritance unless she married by the age of twenty-one. Until then, or if she failed to marry by then, she would receive only an allowance at the discretion of her trustee, Ted. In Ted's absence, Harry had judgment over her allowance, and he threatened to cut her off completely if she failed to get married.

Fiona, who prided herself on being an independent young lady with a mind of her own, found the situation unbearable. She had long since decided she would marry only for love. Having reached the advanced age of twenty without being wed, she had disappointed Cousin Sadie, who considered it her own personal failure for not succeeding in launching her. Fiona had refused a formal coming out in her brother's absence, but even so, there wasn't a lack of offers for her hand. It was well known that she was an heiress in her own right, standing to inherit considerable wealth from her maternal grandmother. Fiona had turned down no fewer than eight offers. To add fuel to the already stressful situation, Harry had started wooing her as well. Fiona had indicated to her cousin that she would only wed when Ted returned. With no news from Ted in months, Harry's offers had become more and more insistent. As Ted never married, Harry was the next in line to inherit his title when Ted died.

"Did I hear mention of an offer?" Cousin Sadie asked as she seated her purple-clad, massive self on the most comfortable chair in the room. She reached for a box of bonbons that rested on an occasional table nearby. "Are congratulations in order?"

"Not quite yet, Mama." Harry smiled at his parent indulgently. "Fiona has only agreed to give some thought to my offer. Isn't that right, Fiona?" Fiona had no chance to object to this before Cousin Sadie started listing all her son's sterling characteristics. It was a list she had heard many times before and could probably recite by heart.

Harry was not a bad-looking man. He was of average height with a slight build and a weak chin. He had light-brown hair that molded his scalp and pale-blue eyes that Fiona always thought looked fishlike. His clothes were always from the best tailors. In addition to both sporting a slight mustache and affecting a monocle, he had taken to wearing many fobs and chains on his person. Therefore, she could be forgiven for thinking him a dandy. She had no intention of ever marrying him; even the thought of it made her sick.

"I am not feeling too well, I think I will go lie down," she said, interrupting Cousin Sadie's monologue, and before her cousin could object, she left the room, closing the door with a decided bang. Making her way upstairs to her room, she closed that door with a louder bang that made Marcie, who was ironing one of her gowns, start and look up in alarm.

"Whatever is the matter, miss?"

"I can't bear it anymore, Marcie." Fiona threw herself into a chair, sighing in frustration. "Cousin Sadie is insufferable and Harry . . ." She paused, looking for an adjective that would best describe her cousin, and not finding one, settled on "slimy."

Marcie stared at her; anxiety written all over her plump face. Fiona, knowing that she had alarmed her maid who was known to have fits of vapors, took a deep breath and forced herself to calm down.

"We are leaving, Marcie. Tomorrow." Fiona sat down at her escritoire and penned a short note in her graceful hand. She folded the note and handed it to Marcie. "Take this to Jim Coachman. Then come back to me posthaste. We have packing to do."

Marcie gaped at her open-mouthed as if two horns had sprouted on her head.

Fiona snapped a finger at her maid. "Off you go. I will explain everything when you return," she said, knowing her maid well enough to know that her curiosity would prevent her from dawdling.

As soon as the door closed behind Marcie, Fiona opened her armoire and started pulling out dresses and hats and laid them on the bed. She would need to prepare for the unpredictable weather.

The carriage wheels jolted over a rut in the road, rousing Fiona from her reverie. *Is it fair to involve Marcie and Jim Coachman in this madcap enterprise?* The question popped into her head as she quelled the increasing anxiety brought on by the impulsive act of running away from her home. What choice did she have? Harry as Ted's heir controlled the purse strings in Ted's absence. In addition, after having had to turn down so many suitors, she had plunged into a self-imposed solitude, as it didn't seem right to enjoy the gaiety of the ton parties when Ted could be dying or worse in some foreign land. She had borne it as long as she could, but Harry's last proposal had been the final straw. Then and there she had decided to run away to Scotland to her maternal uncle's house and remain there until Ted's return. If all went well, she would be in Scotland by the end of the week, safe with her uncle and free of pests such as Harry. *If only I can get there without Harry stopping me, I will be safe. Ted will return soon! I know it!*

The pitter-patter of raindrops interrupted her contemplation. She saw with alarm that the sun, which had heralded their progress until then, had disappeared behind a thick veil of clouds. Hoping it was just a passing storm, she continued to look through the windows at the scenery that turned drab and grey in the dimming light. Her hopes were soon dashed as it turned into a deluge. Winds rocked their little carriage as the weather continued to deteriorate.

Jim Coachman stuck his head in. "Should we stop at the next hostelry and wait it out, miss?"

"No, Jim Coachman. Let's get as far as we can before it gets dark. If the storm continues, we can stop and spend the night at an inn and continue in the morning." She prayed that the storm would soon blow over. If they stopped now, Harry's men might catch up with them and force her to return to London. *I will not go back!*

The carriage traveled on in the rutted, muddy roads, braving the storm. The storm grew in force, and it started to hail. The vehicle was buffeted and shook with the impact of the hailstones. The carriage, which had been going at a reasonable speed, began to slow down. Looking out, Fiona saw that the road was barely visible under the puddles and mud. As she watched, the storm picked up in strength, and the two girls clung to the seats. Thunder cracked around them, and lightning flashed at intervals. Marcie huddled in a corner of the coach with tightly closed eyes, her lips moving as she whispered the same plea over and over: "Oh Lord!"

There was a bright flash followed by a crack like a loud whip and then a resounding crash. Marcie jumped and cowered, quaking like a leaf. Fiona leaned outside in apprehension in time to see the terrified horses rear up, making the carriage lurch. Fiona was hurled across the seat to the other side as the carriage teetered. She felt the vehicle jostle and shudder. *The team has run off the road!* she thought just as her head made contact with the side of the carriage, and she sank into blissful oblivion.

Fiona awoke to a feeling of disembodiment. Rain was falling over her, and she was lying on wet grass. A man, whose hat was dripping water over her face, leaned over her. He was saying something she couldn't quite make out. She tried to raise herself up but sank back when her head swam.

"Stay still, ma'am. You don't appear visibly hurt, but I cannot be sure." The voice sounded authoritative.

Obeying the command, Fiona sank back on the wet ground. She drifted in and out of consciousness. At one point, she was aware of being lifted by strong arms that carried her to a waiting carriage and deposited her on the luxurious seat. Drenched to her skin, Fiona shivered and hugged herself, thankful to be out of the rain. Her head hurt when she tried to recollect what had happened. The carriage door opened, and her rescuer returned, carrying an unconscious Marcie and depositing her gently next to her mistress. The door closed with a snap before she could voice her questions. Fiona peered anxiously at her maid but couldn't see in the dim light if she had been badly hurt. A few minutes later, the carriage door opened yet again, and this time Jim Coachman appeared at the opening, supported by two men. The men helped the battered coachman to a seat and lifted his left leg onto the bench in front of him. In a flash of lightning, Fiona saw the bleeding gash on the elderly retainer's forehead. The coachman moaned softly as he was settled in. After a few more minutes of delay, they were off. Fiona was too tired to question anything, but she noted with gratitude that her rescuer had chosen to ride on the box with his coachman to give them more room inside.

She must have drifted off again, because when she next opened her eyes, the coach had stopped, and there were sounds of activity all around. The carriage door jerked open, and two men appeared in the opening. Without a word to her, they placed supportive arms around a moaning Jim Coachman and helped him down from the carriage. Fiona tried to see where they were taking him, but all she could see was the outline of a distant house in the unrelenting rain. Marcie appeared to be still unconscious. Fiona sat up as another man entered the carriage and prepared to carry Marcie. "Where is this place?" she asked him.

"Crossfields is the home of Lord Sheffield," came the muffled reply as the man and Marcie disappeared from sight.

Fiona sat frozen in shock. *Not Sheffield!* The carriage door opened, and in the dim light, she recognized the man from the Wandering Goose Inn.

"Care to alight, ma'am?" He extended his hand.

She stared at him in consternation. This was quite the pickle to be in. After running away from home to avoid the advances of one rake, she had ended up in the hands of the most notorious rake of all! The man was known to her by reputation only, though at one time he had been a close friend of dear Ted. However, their relationship had suffered, and to make matters worse, Lord Sheffield had wounded Ted in a duel! She quailed at the thought of accepting aid from one such as him.

His smile faltered. "Well, ma'am? I don't have all night."

"Lord Sheffield? I cannot possibly come to your house," she blurted.

"Not overwhelmed by gratitude, I see," he drawled. His sardonic expression told her that he had correctly interpreted her reaction to his identity. "I am not in the mood to ravage muddy, soaked maidens today, so you may be at ease that your virtue is safe with me, ma'am."

Her face reddened further at his crude remarks. "No, you don't understand, sir! I am Fiona Cavendish. Edward Cavendish is my brother."

The man stared at her in disbelief. "Oh! Good God! What a damned mess!" She heard him swear under his breath. Her head hurt, and the shock of the accident made it impossible for her to think straight. She stared at him wordlessly, trying to find a way out of the unbearable situation. He appeared to come to a decision. "There is nothing for it but that you must take shelter at my house tonight."

Fiona shook her head. "No! I will not! My brother will be most distressed. Please take me and my people to the nearest posting house, I beg you."

"Your brother is not here, and you must be addle-witted to suppose that I will allow my coachman or cattle to drive anywhere in this weather. You may have no concern for the well-being of your staff, as is evident in the fact that you chose to be out on the road on a night like this, but I value the lives of my people. I will be damned if I am going to stand in the rain and argue with you. Please alight and let me show you into the house."

Fiona shook her head stubbornly. "I will not set foot in your house willingly, my lord."

"Very well then, let it be noted that you came into my house most unwillingly." Without preamble, he picked her up as if she were a child and carried her from the carriage. A footman hovered beside them, protecting them with an umbrella as his lordship strode purposefully into the house.

Fiona was too surprised to protest until she saw that he was not setting her down in the hall as she expected and instead was carrying her up the stairs. She then struggled furiously against him. "Put me down at once. Where are you taking me?" Her voice sounded querulous to her own ears.

"Why, to bed of course," he replied, innuendo dripping in his cynical voice, and he leered at her dramatically, all the while ignoring her protests and struggles. He strode on up the stairs, not pausing until he reached a door that a footman threw open. He then strode into a bedchamber and deposited her on the bed. With a mocking salute, he turned and left, leaving her to stare openmouthed at the closed door.

Fiona was too stunned to move for some moments. A drop of water dripped from her hair onto her nose and reminded her that she was soaked. Scrambling off the bed, she moved close to the fire that was burning in the hearth. She wasn't sure if it was the cold and wet clothes that made her shiver or the reaction to the day's events.

A little later, a maid appeared with hot water and a very welcome tea tray. "My name's Elsie," she said shyly. "If it pleases you, miss, I can help you out of those wet things, and then you can have this nice tea that Mrs. Pork has sent up just for you."

Elsie matched word to the action, and in no time, Fiona had washed up and was clad in a robe. Elsie then insisted that she get into bed. After the covers were arranged to Elsie's approval, the tea tray was set on the bed with instructions for Fiona to ring if she needed anything, and the maid left Fiona to her tea and thoughts.

After two cups of hot tea, Fiona felt much restored. Too tired to think, she set aside the tea tray, and pulling up the blankets, she nestled into the bed. *I'll deal with his lordship on the morrow. He can't keep me here against my will!* she told herself before she fell asleep.

CHAPTER TWO

Colonel Sir Edward Robert Cavendish, a tall, dark-haired man with the same green eyes as his sister, was not a man who asked for much. An injured man who returned home from war can, however, be excused for expecting a warm welcome. He had taken a musket ball in the war and had not written home, thinking that news of his injury would cause alarm. During the many weeks of pain, he had thought only of his sister and his home, and the goal of seeing them had helped speed up his recovery. He had never been a seafaring man, and the journey back to his homeland had been excruciating. Eager to get home, he had set forth at once from Dover only to be beleaguered by the horrendous storm that had forced him to take shelter longer than he had intended. As a result, he was a day later than anticipated in getting home to his residence in Grosvenor Square. After enduring such a long and wearying journey, Edward Cavendish arrived with no more thought than to sit by his fireplace, enjoy a glass of his excellent brandy, surround himself with his loved ones, and sleep in his own comfortable bed. His knock was answered by Sudbury who, instead of offering the anticipated welcome, blanched and stuttered. "Master Ted!"

This unusual behavior from his usually poker-faced butler alerted him at once that something was amiss.

"Sudbury, what is the matter, man? You look like you've seen a ghost! You did not receive false notice of my death perchance?"

"No, my lord. I am sorry, my lord. Welcome home, my lord." Sudbury bowed, trying to recover his composure. He accepted Ted's traveling cloak and hat, noting with concern that his master looked very wane and hardly in a position to hear the news that awaited him.

"My batman is outside with my horse. Please show him around the stables. He is inclined to not part with me, so please show him every consideration due to my valet."

After Sudbury nodded his assent to this request, Ted advanced into the house in search of refreshment. Entering the drawing-room, Ted was faced with the unappealing prospect of his Cousin Sadie in full lament. When she caught sight of Ted, she made as if to raise herself and sank back instead, as if the very effort was beyond her. Approaching her, Ted offered his cheek for her kiss. Pulling up an ottoman, he sat down near her, holding her trembling hands in his.

"What ails you, my dear cousin?" he asked her. He was flabbergasted to see that his innocent query elicited a cascade of tears and unintelligible words. Cousin Sadie collapsed into sobs, and he was obliged to take her into his arms and allow her to cry against his much-afflicted shoulder until she calmed down.

When the sobs had quieted, he gently set her away and went and rang the bellpull by the fireplace. Sudbury immediately appeared, and Ted requested a strong brandy and a glass of ratafia, which he knew was Cousin Sadie's preferred libation. When Sudbury reappeared shortly with the drinks, Ted approached him. "Where is my sister, Sudbury? Is she not home? Why does she not come to greet her brother?"

This question had the most unfortunate reaction on the old retainer, who was in the act of pouring the brandy. He missed the crystal glass entirely. Golden liquid dripped unheeded onto the ancient, Aubusson carpet as the poor man turned a stricken face to Ted. Gently relieving him of the decanter and setting it down, a now truly alarmed Ted grasped the butler by the shoulders and gave him a gentle shake. "Pull yourself together man!" Staring down the miserable-looking butler in the eye with the haughtiest demeanor imaginable, he demanded, "Sudbury! Enough of this dissembling. Tell me the truth, has something befallen Fiona? Where is she?"

"Miss Fiona is not home, my lord," Sudbury managed to choke out.

"Not home? Where has she gone?"

"We don't know, my lord. Miss Fiona has left home. She departed in the middle of the night with her abigail and Jim Coachman. Master Harry is out looking for her now." The butler looked crestfallen as he made this reluctant revelation.

"What! What is the meaning of this?" Ted thundered, turning to his cousin. The sight of his evident rage made that poor lady rise to her feet. Wringing her hands, she ran to Ted, blubbering incoherently about ungrateful chits and her sweet Harry and her poor heart.

Not able to get a coherent response from her, Ted returned to the brandy decanter and poured himself a good measure and downed it. He was well known in the army for his mercurial temper, and his staff was now introduced to it without further ado. His roar of rage brought the entire household running. After a rigorous questioning of the trembling servants, he had been able to glean the fact that Fiona had taken the coach with their trusted coachman and her abigail a day earlier. Her direction of travel was not clear, but the servants' gossip indicated Scotland.

"She hasn't eloped to Gretna Green, surely!" Ted roared.

The downcast eyes of the staff indicated that they feared she had. Therefore, without staying to get his much-needed rest and respite, Edward immediately ordered for his carriage to be made ready and for his trusted batman, Bates, to pack his Mantons as well as necessities for the journey to Scotland. Then, barely stopping to freshen himself and change his clothes, he left at once in search of his errant sister.

CHAPTER THREE

Fiona rubbed her eyes sleepily and looked around at her surroundings, bemused and disoriented. She was in a pleasant bedchamber, and daylight was peeping in through the pretty, blue drapes at the windows. She stretched her arms and felt a twinge at her shoulder. Memories of the accident and rescue came flooding back in. *I was rescued by Lord Sheffield and am currently in his house.* The thought filled her with consternation, and she sat up abruptly. Her thoughts flew to the state of her companions, which troubled her no less. *I do hope Jim Coachman and Marcie have not sustained a serious injury,* she prayed silently.

Moving and flexing her head and limbs proved that she was for the most part unhurt. While her head felt as if someone had taken a hammer and pounded on it, and her shoulder throbbed a little when she moved it, she did not feel quite as battered as the night before. Fiona was relieved that it was all minor injuries. Just then, the door to her chamber opened, and the maid, who had helped her the previous night, came in. Her cheerful smile put Fiona at ease. Elsie set down the breakfast tray she had brought next to Fiona and drew the curtains aside to let in the daylight. The smell of chocolate and crumpets wafted up, reminding Fiona that she was ravenous. For once foregoing her habit of washing before breakfast, she gratefully accepted a cup of chocolate from the maid.

"Thank you. What is your name?"

"Elsie, miss." The maid bobbed a clumsy curtsy. "I'm the chambermaid, but seeing how your abigail is still doing poorly, Mrs. Pork sent me to help."

"Mrs. Pork?" Fiona bit off a piece of buttery crumpet.

"She's his lordship's housekeeper, miss."

"Is there anyone else in the household?"

"Just the staff, miss."

"My abigail, Marcie, do you know how she's faring?"

"She broke a rib, miss, and is still in bed. It's your coachman who is injured badly, miss, what with the cut on his head and a broken leg."

Fiona choked on her crumpet at this revelation, and Elsie was obliged to thump her on her back with unwonted vigor.

Eyes streaming, Fiona stared at the maid with anxiety. "Oh, dear! That is terrible! I must go see Marcie; she must be worried sick! Poor Jim Coachman must rest. Can we get a doctor in to attend them both?"

"The doctor's been and told your maid to rest. He prescribed laudanum for the coachman, miss."

"Did he say how long Jim Coachman will take to mend?"

"I heard the doctor tell Mrs. Pork that he needed to rest for a few days." Oblivious to the dismay on Fiona's face, Elsie hummed as she rearranged the pillows on the chaise by the window. "That was some accident, miss. I heard the grooms talking about it. Lightning hit a tree in front of your coach and spooked the horses. They ran off the road, and the carriage overturned and ended up in a ditch. It was lucky that the master come upon you on his way back from London. He worked almost an hour in the rain to get you and your maid from inside the carriage. It's a wonder you were not badly hurt, miss. Did you know, miss, that Lord Sheffield personally carried you up into the house? You looked done for, Mrs. Pork said."

Fiona blushed with mortification as she recalled how she had been carried in kicking and screaming. *Of all the people who could have rescued me, why did it have to be him?* Knowing her thoughts to be ungracious, she pushed them away along with her tray; her appetite had dissipated.

When Elsie left promising to return with hot water for a bath, Fiona sank back into her bed feeling fatigued and desolate. Gloom descended on her as she thought about her situation. She knew that Philip Merton, the current, infamous Lord Sheffield, had been her brother's close friend at Eton and had remained his friend even after until they had a falling out over Lady Elizabeth Sheridan. Fiona had been away at finishing school, but Cousin Sadie had spoken of Lady Elizabeth with venom for having chosen Philip Merton over Ted. To hear her say it, Ted had been heartbroken, and his friendship with Merton had suffered. Within a year, Lady Elizabeth had fallen to her death in their London home. There had been an investigation, but Philip's name had been cleared. According to the rumor mills, the ill-fated Lady Elizabeth had been with child at the time of her fall and had died protecting her unborn child from her brute of a husband.

The details were sketchy to Fiona. She knew little of the tragedy, save that Ted and Lord Sheffield had dueled, during which Ted had been seriously injured. His recovery had been slow, and Fiona had feared that her brother would die of his injuries. Philip Merton had retreated to his country seat, Crossfields. That had been nigh five years ago. Since then, he had lived a life of debauchery, if the society pages were to be believed. The stories of his numerous duels and his mistresses had become legendary. Initially, the haut ton had closed their doors to him, and he had not been welcomed in any of the gentlemen's clubs. But not for long. His ailing father's death changed all that. For once he had succeeded his father to the title, the ton had forgiven him, and hopeful mamas now watched his every move in anticipation of marrying their daughters to him. Such was the man whom Fiona was now beholden to. If her reputation had not been completely ruined by running away from home, it surely was now, ensconced as she was in such a notorious man's house.

Her musings were interrupted by Elsie's return, followed by two footmen carrying a hip bath and pails of hot water. The bath revived her, and she found that her portmanteaux had been brought in from the carriage, and her dresses and cosmetics had already been unpacked. Elsie helped her pick out a morning gown. Anxious to go see to her abigail and coachman, Fiona did not linger over her toilette. She found Marcie in a comfortable room, looking rested but still sore.

"Oh! Miss, I am that glad to see you," the tearful maid exclaimed, clasping her mistress's hand. "When I woke this morning in a strange place, I was that scared until Mrs. Pork came and told me that we were rescued by his lordship. Whatever will Mrs. Albrighton say when she finds out that you had to stay at a strange gentleman's home?"

"She will be thankful that we are alive and relatively unharmed." Fiona sounded brisk in an attempt to allay her maid's fears that mirrored her own.

"Not unhurt, miss. I be black and blue all over, with all that jostling and tossing. It is a mercy that my neck isn't broken."

"Oh! Poor Marcie! You'll feel better after some rest." Her heart heavy, she hugged her maid in commiseration and left her still wailing about her ailments.

CHAPTER FOUR

Fiona made her way down the stairs, marveling at her surroundings. Everything around her from the railings to the hardwood floors gleamed as if loving hands had diligently polished and dusted and waxed them every day. The furnishings looked old but suited the house as if they were the true occupants of the mansion. The draperies and art were understated but bespoke luxury and elegance, which was a rare combination. Everything blended and flowed in harmony, undoubtedly chosen with a loving hand and cared for by generations of loving retainers. Fiona noted that the house lacked any feminine touches. There were valuable antique vases scattered everywhere but none had any floral arrangements in them. There was no sign of any handmade laces or embroidery created by a feminine hand. *How strange!*

At the bottom of the stairs, she paused, unsure where to go.

"Good morning, Miss Cavendish. I hope you are feeling better." A stately, old butler had materialized at her elbow. His bald pate gleamed just like the floors, and his brows were thick and grey, but beneath them, a pair of bright, blue eyes sparkled at her. His mouth looked like he was almost about to smile, but never quite made it. He was not a tall man, but his ramrod-straight back made him appear to tower over her diminutive form.

"Yes. Thank you. I am well-rested. Would you be so kind as to direct me to where I may find my coachman, err . . .?"

"My name is Moseley, ma'am. The master wishes to speak with you in the library. If you would please follow me, I will take you there."

He turned and led the way through the house, and she had no choice but to follow. Pausing at an entryway, he knocked smartly and opened the door. "Miss Cavendish to see you, my lord."

Her heartbeat accelerated as she stepped into the library. She found herself in a thoroughly masculine room, with wood-paneled walls lined with bookshelves and a warm fire, around which was grouped a set of comfortable armchairs. In one of these chairs reclined her host, who rose promptly and came to stand before her.

"My lord." Fiona extended her hand.

"Philip Merton at your service," he drawled as he bowed over her hand. Her earlier impression of him from the inn hadn't been false. He was very tall and lean, clothed in an elegantly tailored coat of dark-blue superfine that accented his broad shoulders. His full head of dark, waving hair had been combed back from the highbrow, but a lock had tumbled forward, softening an otherwise severe look. A pair of stony, black eyes beheld her with a cold and cynical expression as they took her measure. He looked about thirty. *Not handsome,* she concluded. Unable to hold his gaze, she looked away, blushing unaccountably.

Philip Merton was far from happy. He had been returning after a trying day in London to meet with his solicitors about the sale of one of his properties when the storm had hit. He'd had to slow down, and it had been extremely late when he neared his estate only to be faced with a wreck. He had jumped out in the storm and, along with his coachman, had toiled for the better part of an hour to pull out the two females from within the carriage. Luckily, the carriage had been intact, but it had toppled into a muddy ditch, making access difficult. By the time he was done rescuing them, he had been thoroughly wet and muddy. Both females and the coachman had to be carried into the house and ministered to. It had been near dawn when, exhausted, he had been allowed to go to bed. Now he was faced with a dilemma. What was he to do with his unexpected and unwelcome guests? Try as he might, he could come up with no satisfactory solution. He was well aware of his own reputation in the ton, and contrary to popular belief, he had no interest in bedding every female he chanced upon, especially not an innocent schoolroom miss! Not that he would ever be attracted to a mousy, grumpy, spoiled chit! Such were his thoughts when his guest was announced.

He glanced up with impatience, and his eyes widened at the transformation that had taken place in the bedraggled, mud-covered girl he had pulled out of the wreckage the previous night. The girl who now approached him was every inch a lady from her glossy, dark hair to her delicate shoes. She was not a beauty in the strictest sense: her mouth was a trifle wide and did not pout as was the latest fashion, and her nose was short and a little upturned at the tip. In the age where golden hair and blue eyes and pouting lips were all the rage, Miss Fiona could only be described as pretty. With wide and disarmingly innocent, green eyes surrounded by thick lashes, along with her tiny frame, it almost made one want to rush to be her champion and protect her from the big, bad world.

Stopping the line of his thoughts, he gave himself a mental shake for indulging in flights of fancy, and that over a chit who looked like she belonged in the schoolroom. This was Ted's little sister, whom Ted used to refer to as "chick" in their Eton days. What would Ted say if he knew that she was now in his house and without a chaperone? He would call him out, and there would be another disastrous duel. It just wouldn't do. It would be best to send her on her way as soon as possible.

He was amused to note that she was visibly flustered by his bold appraisal, but when she spoke, she sounded anything but meek. "Lord Sheffield, my staff and I are very indebted to you for coming to our aid yesterday."

"Please don't mention it, Miss Cavendish. I am glad to see that you are looking well and that I could be of some assistance."

"Can you please tell me how my coachman fares?"

"I am sorry to have to inform you that your coachman has suffered a broken leg. The doctor from the village has been in, and he has advised that he not be moved for several days. Your abigail too has suffered some severe injuries and needs to rest. May I inquire as to your destination so that your family may be informed?" He noted how her eyes widened in apparent distress at his news. Seeing her appalled face and guessing that his reputation was the reason for her reluctance to accept any aid from him, he grew more cynical.

"I understand your predicament, Miss Cavendish. If you give me your direction, I will have my coachman and grooms convey you to your destination as soon as you can travel, while your servants recuperate. That may be the best solution, as this is a bachelor domicile, and your unchaperoned presence here will surely cause comment." He spoke coldly and was pleased to note that she had the grace to blush.

"I thank you, my lord, but I was traveling to visit relatives in Scotland. My cousin in London, who is my current guardian, is doing poorly, and I do not want to distress her further. If I may impose on you to take me to the local hostelry until my servants can travel, I would be most grateful."

Philip could only stare at her as if she had sprouted horns. "I am afraid that's quite impossible, Miss Cavendish. I can hardly leave an unchaperoned young lady at the local hostelry. It's out of the question."

She looked like she was about to argue, but after a moment in which he saw many fleeting expressions flit across her expressive eyes, she gave in with poor grace. "Very well, then, I must beg that you let me remain here until my servants can travel. I will accept your offer to have your staff escort me once my coachman can accompany me." Her voice betrayed her vexation with the situation.

Philip heard the displeasure in her voice and was riled, but he could hardly force her to leave. "I'm delighted to have such an enchanting guest grace my home." He bowed, and his voice conveyed his sarcasm. "My housekeeper, Mrs. Pork, will serve as sufficient chaperone under the circumstances. Do you desire that word should be sent to your relatives about your delay in reaching Scotland?"

There was another pause, as a warring expression on her face spoke of an internal dilemma, before she said, "That is truly kind, my lord. I will write a letter to my uncle this afternoon, if you would be so kind as to frank it for me."

Philip bowed again. He sensed that she wasn't being completely honest and had not given him the whole truth. There was little he could do but hope that once her letter reached her relatives, they would come and escort her away.

Fiona left the library and returned to her room to write the letter. She could not very well ask her family to come and escort her to Scotland, and neither could she ask Uncle Henry for help, as he was unaware of her plans to visit him. Now she was forced to remain in the home of Lord Sheffield! What a predicament to be in! With no other recourse, knowing he expected her to write a letter, she wrote a brief note to Uncle Henry inquiring after his health but did not mention her escapade. She then gave the letter to a footman to give to his lordship.

Gloom settled on her, and her room felt claustrophobic. She tried to make her way to the library again in the hope of getting a book to read. On reaching the stairs, she found housemaids busy dusting and polishing, and not wanting to disturb them, she retreated and decided to look for the back stairs. Her nose guided her to the kitchen, from where delicious smells were emanating. She thought to look in on the cook and housekeeper to thank them for their care of Jim Coachman and Marcie and to see if she could help.

Pushing open the doors to the kitchen, she stepped in, startling the kitchen maid, who shrieked and promptly dropped a pot of potatoes. The shriek, in turn, scared the scullery maid, who dropped the kettle of hot water she was carrying. The kitchen cat shot up from the windowsill, where he had been napping, and scrambled through the door, with his hair standing on end, between the legs of Moseley, who just then arrived to investigate. Moseley fell heavily and landed on his rump with a loud yelp. Two older women, whose apparel indicated that they were the cook and the housekeeper, came running. The cook slipped in the water on the floor and collapsed on top of the butler with an ear-rending shriek. The housekeeper skid on the potatoes and ended up on top of the cook with a bellow. The resulting cacophony of crashes coupled with shrill voices caused the master of the house, and every footman within earshot, to come posthaste to the scene of the calamity.

Fiona wished that the earth would open up and swallow her whole as she watched Lord Sheffield's eyebrows rise almost to his hairline, and his brow creased up in deep furrows at the sight of the mess in the kitchen. Petrified, she stood helpless amid the chaotic scene, while he and the footmen briskly disentangled butler, housekeeper, and cook and sent them off to change into dry clothes with soothing words that did little to soothe the injured dignity of those good people. The scullery maid and kitchen maid were asked to clean up the mess on the floor. His lordship then turned to confront the shamefaced offender as she blushed a deep red. Without a word, he placed a firm hand under her elbow and escorted her firmly from the kitchen. Surprised at this cavalier treatment, Fiona found her tongue at last and tried to explain her role in the mishap. Her faltering sentences fell on deaf ears. Without a pause, he marched her out, and once they were outside the library, her host bade her a curt good day and disappeared within closed doors before she could ask if she could borrow a book.

She stood fuming outside the library for many minutes. His high-handed manner grated on her nerves. Taking several deep breaths, she looked about her, finding more maids and footmen busy about their business who all peeped at her with curiosity and some with amusement as word of her kitchen escapade spread. Feeling disconsolate and decidedly underfoot, she wallowed for a minute in self-pity. She thought about returning to her room to fetch her bonnet and shawl but decided not to walk past the furtively grinning household staff. The gardens that she glimpsed through the open doors appealed to her bruised ego, and she stepped through the doors with her head held high.

Sunlight greeted her, and all around she saw gardeners busy cleaning up the ravages of the storm from the picturesque and rambling grounds. Standing outside in the courtyard, she looked back at the house and marveled anew at the beautiful architecture. There were influences of Gothic and Baroque styles. The center of the mansion entry had a dramatic projection with sprawling wings on both sides. The construction was of white stone that now looked grey with the ravages of age and sported the occasional sculptural and decorative motif, which was there purely for ornamentation. *How splendid it all is!* she thought, admiring the immense structure and its surroundings.

Spotting the stables in the distance, she walked briskly in their direction to inquire whether her team had been severely injured in the accident. She found the stables a hive of activity.

"Can I be of assistance, miss?" one of the grooms stopped his work to ask.

"I was just worried about my horses. Were they injured badly in the accident yesterday?"

"No, miss, apart from being badly frightened, they did not suffer any harm."

Noting that the stable hands had stopped their work to gawk at the unusual female presence and feeling awkward at the unwanted attention, Fiona did not linger and left the stables to stroll toward the gardens.

The garden, like the house, was neat and well planned in a riot of color. Every plant, shrub, and tree had been chosen with care and had been methodically and lovingly tended. The rose gardens were painted every hue. Taking in a lungful of fresh air and breathing in the scent of the fragrant blossoms soothed Fiona's frayed nerves. She strolled about enjoying the feel of the sun on her face. Admiring the borders with the lavender and the lilies and irises in every shade of the rainbow gave her an idea. What better way to show gratitude to her host and his staff than by placing some well-arranged floral decorations in the masculine, albeit beautiful, house? Spotting a gardening shed close to the back of the house, she ventured there to borrow shears and a basket and set to work. Soon she had collected enough blooms to fill a dozen vases. Returning the shears, she carried her basket proudly into the house. Meeting Moseley, who had recovered his poise, she asked where she could work on the flower arrangements. He looked dubious and like he was about to object, but the firm look of determination in her eye stayed him, and he guided her to a little room next to the kitchen, where she found a worktable. Moseley absented himself briefly and returned with a variety of vases.

Fiona prided herself in being an adept hand at creating floral arrangements, and the morning flew past at she busied herself in creating her masterpieces. It was with a distinct feeling of satisfaction that she enlisted the help of the footmen to distribute them around the house. Roses for the parlor. Irises for the foyer. Lilies for the library. And her pièce de résistance: a mixed floral bouquet of impressive dimensions for the dining room.

She carried this last arrangement in a priceless Waterford vase herself and followed the footman to the dining room. Setting the vase down with infinite care, she stepped back to admire her handiwork. Her eye for detail spotted that one of the flowers needed a little adjustment, and she proceeded to do just that and, in the process, woke a bee that had been slumbering, hidden inside the bloom. The bee buzzed around furiously and alighted on her hand. Fiona tried to shake the bee off by waving her hand but instead connected with the vase and sent it crashing, spewing flowers and water all over the table and floor. The infuriated bee stung her for good measure and buzzed away through an open window. Fiona stood in the middle of her ruined masterpiece, close to tears at her ruined efforts and aghast at destroying the priceless vase. She held her smarting arm, which had become red and started to swell like a tomato.

The second crash in as many hours brought the master storming from the study, where he had been trying to balance his accounts, accompanied by Moseley and several footmen.

"What is the meaning of this?" His roar made her quake in her shoes, and she had to blink back the impending tears.

His icy survey took in the scene of disaster in the dining room. A snap of his fingers set the footmen to cleaning up the broken glass and the flowers before he turned to Fiona.

"Miss Cavendish, would you please accompany me?"

Without waiting for her response, he turned and headed into the library, with Fiona trailing behind him. Once ensconced in that room with the door closed and out of earshot of the servants, he turned on her. His face resembled a thunder cloud, and the thinning of his lips was an indication that his temper was being held severely in check.

"Miss Cavendish, while I appreciate your enthusiasm and attachment to flowers, I must ask you to refrain from playing with them again," he began, then stopped to grope and fish out a handkerchief.

Tears pricking her eyelids, hand smarting with pain, Fiona bowed her head and whispered, "I am sorry, my lord, I was only trying to show my gratitude to you and your staff by brightening up your house with the flowers. But the b—"

Achoo! She was interrupted by a huge sneeze from his lordship, who emerged from his handkerchief with a red nose and watering eyes.

"Miss Cavendish, my staff and I genuinely appreciate your gesture, but there is no question of gratitude. Please do not feel that you must repay us on any account. In fact, I positively forbid you to mention it again." He wheezed. "I will be—"

What he would be was never discovered, as he succumbed to a sneezing fit. When the sneezing subsided, she saw him glare at the vase of lilies with watering eyes. Dismay made her gasp as he grabbed the vase and marched up to the door and flung it open. A footman, who looked like he had just sprung back from having his ear at the door, hastened to take the offending article from his seething lordship.

"Get rid of this rubbish," Philip said succinctly before the door closed on the startled footman's face.

Fiona, who had stood frozen through that entire savage act, quailed when he grabbed her arm and attempted to shepherd her to the door. An involuntary cry of pain escaped her lips as his fingers closed over her stinging arm. He released her at once. His eyes widened, and he blanched in apparent horror when he saw the red, swollen appendage.

"Miss Cavendish, I am truly sorry. I did not realize that you had been hurt. Is it a bee sting?"

Fiona nodded, not trusting herself to speak for fear the tears would come out.

"The stinger must be removed immediately; will you permit that I remove it?" A quick tug to the bellpull was followed by instructions for Mrs. Pork to bring some cold water for the bee sting. Then he led her to the window and seated her gently on the chair that was placed there, and kneeling in front of her, he held her elbow with one hand while he squeezed the stung skin between the finger and thumb of the other. Fiona winced and squeezed her eyes closed but did not cry out. It was quite unexpected when she felt his lips on her injured arm. Her pain was forgotten as her skin tingled with new awareness. His lips felt warm and moist as he tried to suck out the stinger. It awakened hitherto unknown sensations within her. Her eyes flew open, and she gazed startled at the man who could invoke such sensations at a mere touch. Her eyes became glazed while she looked on in fascination at his downbent head as he strived against the offending stinger.

"I got it." Fiona almost felt bereft when he withdrew his mouth from her skin and looked up at her to meet her eyes. For the life of her, she couldn't look away. He remained on his knees, gazing back at her, his expression blank, still holding her hand in his.

A knock on the door made him spring to his feet and beat a rapid retreat from the library. Startled by his sudden departure, Fiona stared befuddled at the matronly, grey-haired, diminutive woman who entered the library with a tea tray and a glass of cold water, as well as a jar of honey. She recognized one of the women who had been victims of the earlier disaster in the kitchen and flushed in mortification.

"We haven't been formally introduced, Miss Cavendish. I'm Mrs. Pork, the housekeeper here." She smiled kindly at Fiona as she poured her a cup of tea.

Fiona smiled back and accepted the tea gratefully. While she sipped the refreshing beverage, Mrs. Pork bathed the afflicted arm with cool water and applied a little honey to it. Her ministrations were remarkably effective, and soon the pain and swelling had reduced. Far from feeling better, Fiona felt more tearful by her kindness. Overcome by the multitude of disasters that had followed her since she left home, her control broke down, and her tears crept unheeded down her face. Her distress affected Mrs. Pork, who enfolded her in her motherly arms and patted her shoulder as Fiona wept out her frustrations. It wasn't long before she found herself pouring out all her woes, starting with her running away from home and ending with the disaster with the bee.

"And after all my hard work, he asked the footman to throw away my flowers!" She sobbed, that fact having hurt more than the bee sting.

"It's not like Lord Sheffield to do something like that," Mrs. Pork mused aloud, shaking her head. "Indeed, he doesn't care for flowers, but usually he has impeccable manners, and that doesn't seem like him at all . . . unless . . . they weren't lilies, were they?" She looked at Fiona with a query in her eyes.

"Yes, as a matter of fact, they were," Fiona replied querulously. "Does he especially despise them?"

"No, my dear, but they give him hay fever. Has been afflicted by them ever since he was a little boy in short coats. One whiff of them is enough to make him sneeze and his eyes water, and he gets a bad headache too."

Fiona remembered the horrendous sneezes that had cut off her attempt to apologize and felt guilty. *Everything is going wrong!* Instead of expressing her gratitude as intended, she had caused her host considerable discomfort, not to mention the damage to his priceless vase.

Her eyes threatened to tear up again when Mrs. Pork patted her comfortingly. "There, there, child. You weren't to know. His lordship isn't one to hold it against you, especially after all you've been through."

Her words made Fiona sit upright. "Mrs. Pork, please don't tell him that I ran away from home. He will make me go back, and I can't marry

Cousin Harry. Please."

Mrs. Pork hesitated as she looked at her, considering. "I will not lie to my employer if he asks me directly, but if he doesn't, I don't see why I should seek him out and tell him."

With that, Fiona had to be content. She thanked Mrs. Pork for her kindness and declined to have lunch sent to her room.

CHAPTER FIVE

Philip Merton sat fuming and irritable as he stared at the estate books in his study. That morning he had been trying to check the estate accounts before meeting with his bailiff and had been interrupted by one disaster after the other. And the underlying cause of each mishap had been Miss Fiona Cavendish. The girl who had dared to disdain his hospitality last night and had infuriatingly refused to leave this morning. He had known from the first that she spelled trouble with a capital T, and his prediction had been accurate. He had tried to avoid her company but had been forced into it by her predilection for disaster. And now he had a headache from the darn lilies she had placed in his study just to torment him. Most importantly, he had no clue what to do about her. He didn't want her in his house. She was a girl just out of the schoolroom, not to mention the sister of a man who hated him. He had never met her during the days when he had enjoyed Ted's friendship, for she had been away at a seminary. And then Ted and he had grown apart due to the turn of events.

The thought of those events made him frown. Just being associated with him was enough to ruin her. But in all conscience, he could not turn her out either. He had noted the direction of the letter she had sent off that morning and decided that if no one came to fetch her in a day or two, he would ride out to Scotland himself and bring someone back with him. It would have been much easier if Ted had not been cavorting about the continent playing soldier. Philip never would have guessed when he injured Ted in that duel that in a few years' time he would be desperately wishing for the man's safe return so he could take his darn nuisance of a sister off Philip's hands.

Amid all these negative thoughts, the picture of guileless, green eyes that had looked so dejected earlier intruded, making him pause. She had been more distressed by the broken vase and the flowers he had thrown away than the pain of the bee sting in her hand. The memory of the chaos she had wrought so innocently and in such a short time brought a reluctant smile to his eyes. That she cared enough about her servants to delay her journey for them was commendable. He thought about how pretty she had looked when she came to see him that morning. Her sweet and delicate fragrance had teased his senses. Her skin had felt like silk under his fingers and mouth. It had taken all of his self-control to resist the urgent need to pull her into his arms and shower her with caresses. Her wondering and innocent look that seemed to delve into the depths of his soul had almost undone him. Only Mrs. Pork's timely arrival had prevented him. He shook his head as if to push away such thoughts and returned to his ledger. Only to be interrupted yet again by the object of his thoughts entering his study unannounced.

Philip rose swiftly to his feet as Fiona swept into his study. She came to a halt in front of him.

"My lord, I am sorry to have caused you discomfort. I did not know that you were afflicted by lilies, or I would never have brought them into the house. I only meant to cheer up the rooms, but instead I have caused more harm than good. I hope you are not too discomposed by my efforts." She looked the picture of maidenly contrition, and Philip was taken aback by this sincere apology. There was no sign of the aversion she had displayed that morning. Her face was genuinely contrite and reflected concern. The firm set down he was about to give her when she'd entered unannounced died prematurely on his lips.

To his own surprise, he found himself rushing to assuage her feelings. "Miss Cavendish, it is I who should apologize for speaking so harshly to you earlier when you were already hurting from the bee sting. I pray you will excuse my bad manners. May I inquire if your poor arm is better?"

"Yes, thank you, my lord. Mrs. Pork has very kindly ministered to it. I realize that my presence in your house is an inconvenience, and I will stay out of your way for the duration of my stay here."

"On the contrary, Miss Cavendish. My home is honored by your presence, and I hope you will do whatever you must to be comfortable here. And I hope you will grace my table with your presence at dinner this evening." Philip was more surprised than she by his impulsive invitation.

Her eyes widened at this, and she looked at him uncertainly. Then a small smile crept to her lips, followed by the flush that made her cheeks pink as a tiny dimple appeared there.

"Thank you, my lord. I would like that." She curtsied gracefully and left him. Alone, Philip wondered what had come over him to ask her to dine with him. He shook his head ruefully; it was too late to withdraw his invitation now, but perhaps he could use the opportunity to persuade her to leave his house before her reputation was subjected to any damage.

CHAPTER SIX

Philip remained in a pensive mood as he dressed for dinner. One part of him was looking forward to seeing Fiona again. Another part acknowledged that his feelings of anticipation could only bode trouble. He reluctantly admitted to himself that he was more attracted to her than he had been to any other woman in a long while. No good would come of the attraction. He was a jaded widower with a reputation that, though largely rumor and conjecture, was nevertheless believed by most of the ton. She was a mere innocent, and any association with him would hurt her. Honor dictated that he should keep his distance from her. It had been so long since he had any company at Crossfields, and even though he was loath to admit it, his life recently had been lonely. *Could I not enjoy one evening in her company? Would that be so bad? She is already here, and any damage to her reputation already done, how could dining with her do more harm? What nonsense! If I had any brains at all, I would distance myself from her before it was too late. No, better yet! Be kind and treat her like the child that she is and persuade her to leave as quickly as possible.*

Fiona dressed with great care that evening. A much-recovered Marcie and Elsie together assisted her and styled her hair into a cluster of curls that cascaded down one shoulder. After a lot of indecision, she finally chose a gown of deep-green silk edged with cream lace at the bodice and sleeves. She told herself that the dress gave her confidence, and she desperately needed it since every encounter with her host had left

33

her feeling immature and inadequate. She wanted to appear beautiful and sophisticated for once so he wouldn't treat her like an indulged debutante. Her heart beat faster as her mind dwelled on her host. The memory of his lips on her skin as he drew out the bee sting made her cheeks grow warm and flush to a pretty rose color. Her fingers trembled as she fastened high-heeled shoes, chosen specially so she wouldn't feel quite so short in his presence. As she caught up a pretty, embroidered shawl in her arm and made her way downstairs for dinner, she smiled in anticipation of seeing him again. Would he notice her appearance? Would he pay her a compliment as she acknowledged she wanted him to do so very badly? Or would he dismiss her again as a silly chit?

Moseley announced her into the well-appointed and tastefully furnished parlor. The silk jacquard drapes were drawn, and a roaring fire added to the coziness of the room. The bright candles flickered merrily, throwing shadows on the muted Aubusson rugs. A large portrait of a distinguished man standing behind a beautiful, blonde-haired woman, both dressed in the style of a past decade, hung over the mantelpiece and dominated the room. Her host stood by the fireplace, leaning against the marble mantel, swirling cognac in a sparkling, crystal glass, staring into the flickering flames. The resemblance between the man in the portrait and the man who stood beneath it was so remarkable that she concluded they must be father and son. One look at him impeccably dressed in midnight-blue and silver took her breath away.

Gazing at him shyly, she stepped into the room as the door closed behind her. He moved forward as she attempted to glide nonchalantly toward him like she had seen taller women than herself do, but alas, her high heels caught in the fringe of her shawl and pitched her forward abruptly. In a lightning move, he leapt forward and caught her before she fell. She found herself clasped tightly against a hard-masculine chest, enveloped by strong arms, and with her nose pressed against a snowy and expertly tied cravat. She was again enticed by his distinct masculine aroma of soap mixed with cognac, which made her feel deliciously lightheaded. She could hear his heartbeat close to her, and the rhythm somehow made her feel safe in his arms, as if she belonged there. Did she imagine it or did his heart race as he held her? She glanced up at him in confusion and saw him looking down at her, his eyes like deep, mesmerizing pools, yet ever so eloquent in an unspoken message. They gazed at her as if seeking and yearning for something beyond his reach. She was reluctant to step away and stayed in his embrace, reveling in being held as if she were infinitely precious. It was with reluctance that she let go of him and stepped away. He left her and made his way back to the mantelpiece, where he had left his glass, and remained there with his back slightly to her, giving her the time, she needed to regain her composure.

Fiona felt strangely bereft and, shivering, stayed fixed to the spot, her mind filled with a dizzying swirl of emotions. Then, recalling her clumsy entrance, her face flushed a deep crimson in confusion and mortification. *So much for being sophisticated! I literally fell into his arms! Whatever must he think of me? That I am setting my cap for him?* That thought made her burn and cringe, and she resolved to disabuse him of such notions by being cool and reserved for the duration of the evening. When she had taken a deep breath and composed herself, she stepped forward, and he returned to usher her to a seat and offer her a glass of ratafia. With her resolution in place, Fiona felt self-conscious of every syllable that passed her lips, and her conversation was stilted at best and nonexistent at worst. After they had covered mundane topics such as the weather and the terrible state of the roads, she lapsed into an uncomfortable silence.

It was almost a relief to be summoned to dinner. At first, the conversation at the dinner table was nonexistent as well. Philip looked bored and continued to treat her as he would a much younger and not particularly liked niece. This rankled, and she acted as if talking to him caused her profound discomfort and focused on getting through the meal. The cook had outdone herself, and Fiona, blessed with a healthy appetite, found herself enjoying the food. In between the sumptuous and mouthwatering courses, Moseley poured a deep, burgundy wine into their glasses. To hide her nervousness, Fiona drank her glass down in a gulp, hoping to gain enough courage to last out the evening with dignity. Moseley discreetly refilled it again and then again. Being unaccustomed to drinking so much wine, she lost some of her reserve. Her eyes wandered the dining room with renewed interest. She took in the intricately carved and molded ceilings, the ornate mirrors on the walls, and the magnificent chandelier with awe. She looked up to see her host watching her, his eyebrows raised in apparent amusement.

"Has this house been in your family long?" Her voice betrayed her interest.

"Yes. Three generations, I am the fourth."

"It's wonderful, how it has retained its air of antiquity. It has a distinct Baroque influence; has it ever been redecorated?"

"Several times, the last by my mother. In fact, every countess of Sheffield has managed to retain the original style in their choice of furnishings and made it their own."

"How original! Who was the first countess who lived here?"

"Her name was Lady Carolina, and according to family history, she was the daughter of a Spanish lord. My great-grandfather, Philip Merton, the second Earl of Sheffield, swept her off her feet on a trip to Spain and brought her back here. He built this house for her and incorporated some Spanish style into the architecture and décor to make her feel at ease in England away from her warm, Mediterranean home."

It was the most she had heard him speak, and the transformation in his face when animated by conversation was fascinating.

"What a beautiful story!" Fiona smiled at him, entranced by the romance, forgetting her resolve to be distant.

"I am not sure that it's the whole truth. I suspect in reality my ancestor was a pirate and made off with the Spanish lady during his travels. When through circumstance he inherited the title, I think my family modified his story to make our heritage more respectable." His eyes danced with humor as they looked at her.

Fiona looked at him sharply. "Even so, he must have loved her dearly to have built this mansion for her. It reminds me of the story of the emperor who built the Taj Mahal in India."

"You mean Shah Jahan? I've read that he was hotheaded and rebelled against his own father, no less."

Fiona's eyes sparked in outrage. "Must you spoil every story, my lord?"

"No, I just couldn't resist. You were so carried away by the romance." His smile was so dazzling that she had to blink. *How could I think him anything but handsome?*

Before she could recover, he asked, "How is it that a sheltered young lady like you is so well versed in Mughal history?"

"Why is it so unusual for a lady to take an interest in other cultures?"

she countered.

"It is my experience that ladies prefer to shop and talk about the latest on dit rather than read about foreign cultures."

"Then your experience must be very limited. Most young ladies are well versed in art, music, and history."

"Is that so? The young misses I have come across like to simper and flirt but not converse."

"They are probably afraid to intimidate you with their wit." He grinned at this hit, and again she was mesmerized.

"So, tell me, Miss Cavendish, what other hobbies do you pursue? Is it possible that you number a knowledge of politics among your many talents?"

"Why is that so hard to imagine? Should a woman not have an opinion about the government which sets her rights? Do all women have to be as empty-headed and silly as you gentlemen imagine?"

"Au contraire, I think women's voices should be heard and that the inequality between the sexes should be removed in all walks of life, including politics."

Used to the gentlemen who thought a well-read woman a bluestocking and that women should not involve their "pretty little heads" about such matters as politics, she could only stare at him in surprise.

"What is it, Miss Cavendish? Are you guilty of casting all men in the same chauvinistic mold?" His eyes twinkled, and he looked younger and more carefree just then.

The ice was broken, and the rest of the evening sped by. She found that her interest in arts, music, and literature was mirrored by his own. He did not spare her by agreeing to all she said, as she was accustomed, and instead they engaged in a lively discussion on the merits of impressionist art and foreign policy. His laughter rang out repeatedly when she shared funny anecdotes about her time at the ladies' finishing school, and he matched her story for story with anecdotes from his own youth. When it was time for Fiona to leave him to his port, he rose graciously as she left the room with reluctance.

Fiona made it to the pianoforte in the music room where she ran her fingers over the keys, hoping he wouldn't be long. She found a song she knew and sat down to play it. She played lightly at first and then with a more upbeat tempo, singing softly along. Looking up, she found him standing at the door watching her. A crimson blush tinted her face, and she stopped abruptly.

"Please don't stop. That was lovely," he said as he came to join her.

She finished playing the song with him standing next to her listening.

"Thank you," he said when she was done. "That was one of my mother's favorites, and I haven't heard it in ages."

"Do you play, my lord?"

"I have been known to pick out a few tunes." The corner of his mouth quirked up.

"Let's see if we can find something we both know, then you can accompany me."

Soon she was singing to his accompaniment as unaffectedly as she did most things. Her voice was clear and true if not strong, and he played well. When he played a duet, she was surprised to hear his baritone join her soprano in the chorus. Glancing over her shoulder when they finished, she was further surprised to see his servants gathered outside the door to listen. Mrs. Pork and the cook were both wiping tears from their eyes. Moseley looked a bit misty as well.

She found herself basking in Philip's presence, and when he suggested a stroll in the garden, she accepted eagerly. He called for her shawl and draped it over her shoulders, offered her his arm, and led her to the rose garden. It was a clear, cloudless night. The stars were shining brightly overhead, and the garden looked magical in the moonlight. The nightly creatures were making music, and the fragrance of roses was everywhere. Philip bestowed his full attention on her, and his effortless charm entranced her. She came to life in his company. She was unaware of what they spoke or where they wandered, delighting only in his presence. She knew not what drew her to him; was it the danger of the unknown? The lure of his reputation? No, it was deeper than that. For the first time in her young life, she felt she was free to speak and behave without being judged or trying to impress. She felt a connection to him that she could not identify but could sense went deeper than their brief acquaintance, woven into the very fabric of their being. They understood each other in a way that words could not describe. As trust and other feelings took hold of her young heart, Fiona was content to spend the evening with her host. Their peaceful interlude was, however, rudely interrupted by a most unexpected sound.

Fiona clutched at Philip's arm. "Do you hear that, my lord?" she asked.

Philip cocked his head to one side and listened, and then he too heard it. A faint mewling. It seemed to be coming from a nearby tree. Philip made his way to the tree with Fiona in tow, making haste but little sound. Looking up, he saw the source of the noise.

"Oh! Look, it's a kitten!" Fiona cried. "Poor little thing! It's stuck up in the tree and can't get down."

Philip stared at the little creature for a minute. "If you will excuse me a moment, Miss Cavendish," he said, divesting himself off his coat and cravat.

In a trice, he was up the tree, climbing nimbly until he had reached the hapless creature. He reached his hand to it, but the frightened kitten shot out a tiny paw and scratched his outstretched hand. Fiona heard him curse succinctly, and then he had the creature tucked securely in the crook of his arm as he made his way back down.

Fiona took the tiny kitten from him and held its shivering body to herself, crooning soft caresses to it. "Look, my lord, isn't it the most darling creature?" she queried, dimpling up at him with innocent eyes. Philip grinned in amusement as he retrieved his discarded garments. "Come along then, Miss Cavendish, let's find your "most darling creature" some food and a place for the night," he said, offering her his arm.

Together they made their way back into the house and to the kitchen. The surprised staff, who were sitting at the kitchen table taking their well-deserved rest and refreshment, sprang to their feet at the sight of the master in shirtsleeves accompanied by the girl clutching a kitten.

"Sorry to interrupt your evening, please be at ease. Miss Cavendish would like a saucer of cream for her little friend," Philip said with an endearing smile.

In a jiffy, many hands came to the kitten's aid, and it was soon curled up by the kitchen fire, replete after a good meal of thick cream. After a last look at her protégé, Fiona took his lordship's arm and accompanied him back to the drawing room.

Philip poured her a drink and another for himself. Their eyes met as he handed her the glass, and they both burst out in unconstrained laughter.

"Oh! Their faces," Philip gasped between peals.

"They couldn't believe their eyes!" Fiona chortled, clutching his arms as tears of mirth rolled down her face.

"You will never live this down," said Fiona. "The master in soiled shirtsleeves and a kitten, it's a tale they will tell their children and grandchildren for years." And she set them off again.

"Moseley and Mrs. Pork probably have several such stories from my childhood capers. I bet they are going to start telling those now," said Philip, sobering. He caught sight of the twinkle in Fiona's eyes and couldn't help joining her in another round of mirth.

After that, they traded childhood scrapes in unabashed fashion; all decorum was forgotten as they reveled in outdoing one another in relating naughty escapades. It was well after midnight when they returned to the house, and Philip led Fiona to the stairs. She offered her hand and bade him good night, but instead of bowing over it, he raised it to his lips and kissed it, his eyes looking at her with a strange intensity. Fiona shivered unaccountably at the caress and gazed back at him in wonder. Intoxicated by his nearness and mesmerized by the look in his eyes, she swayed and leaned toward him. His eyes dropped to her mouth, and his own hovered a mere inch or two above hers. Her breath became shallow, and her heart beat a little faster, fluttering in tandem with the million butterflies that had suddenly awoken in her belly. *He's going to kiss me!* The thought thrilled her, and her eyes fluttered closed in anticipation, her pulse beating a rapid tattoo at the hollow of her neck.

"Good night, Miss Cavendish!" Philip let her hand go and stepped back. He bowed once and then abruptly turned and walked back to his study.

For a moment, Fiona stood at the base of the staircase, disoriented by his brusque departure. After some lonely moments, she slowly turned and, dragging her feet, made her way upstairs to her room. She dismissed the sleepy Marcie, changed out of her gown and into her night rail, and prepared for bed. Sleep eluded her for a long time, and so she went and sat by the window to cool her hot cheeks all the while a smile playing on her lips. She thought of the delightful evening she had just spent with Philip. His velvety eyes dominated her thoughts as she relived the feeling of smooth lips against her skin, and she shivered. Then the voice of reason intervened and interrupted her pleasant fantasy.

He is an experienced rake, and if rumor holds true, a libertine as well. He is obviously experienced in the art of seduction. How foolish to be taken in by his charm. Men such as him wanted only one thing from gullible girls, and it wasn't her heart. *Yet he had not so much as stolen a kiss. He was nothing but a perfect gentleman,* her heart wailed. Wasn't the man who had exerted so much charm that evening the very same who had caused Ted to become an invalid for so long? Hadn't he in addition also abused and killed his wife? *I can't believe that of him! Surely he is not capable of such evil. I would know if he was a scoundrel!* her heart persisted. And what of Ted? Was he not to be considered? Had he not called Sheffield out? Ted must have had good reason to do so, and to deny that would be disloyal to her brother. Reason argued and won. Fiona desolately turned away from the window, deciding she would do well to keep away from him until she could depart his house. The thought did little to comfort her restlessness, and though she went to bed, sleep evaded her until the early hours of the morning. When at last she fell into a fitful slumber, she dreamed of being kissed by a dark man with velvety eyes, and she was wantonly begging for more.

The next morning, Fiona woke up late. Marcie brought her chocolate and toast with jam in bed. On her breakfast tray, she found a note from Philip. He apologized that he had to leave her alone while he had to go to a neighboring estate to meet up with friends for a long-planned visit. He requested that she make herself at home and ask his staff for anything that may make her stay comfortable. He signed himself her humble servant. Marcie informed her that Lord Sheffield had left at dawn. The staff was told not to wait up for him that evening, as he was planning to dine with his friends.

His departure was like an anticlimax. Forgetting her own resolve of staying away from him, she was contrarily disappointed and peeved that he had chosen to go away and leave her alone. It had begun to rain by the time she went downstairs, as if the weather were mirroring her doldrums, and this did nothing to improve her somber mood. When she tried to seek further information from Moseley on her host's whereabouts, Fiona was informed that he was attending a house party hosted by Sir Cameron Langton.

"His lordship has known Sir Cameron since they were together at Eton. Lord Hector Bainbridge will be there as well," Moseley imparted with a fatherly smile. Fiona assimilated this piece of information with surprise. She knew both Lord Bainbridge and Sir Langton to be friends of Ted. Sir Cameron was an honorable man with great connections and a reputation for integrity who was well-received everywhere. Lord Bainbridge was one of the much sought-after bachelors of the ton, as he was both rich and connected. Fiona fondly recalled the handsome, blond-haired and blue-eyed Corinthian who had been one of her suitors, until she had told him that she was waiting for Ted's return. At which point he had graciously relegated himself her escort, when possible, but had not pushed his suit, for which she was grateful. He was invited to all the ton events, so that had been a frequent and happy occurrence, as it served to keep her other suitors at bay.

Fiona's heart, which had been subdued by her ponderings of the night before, fluttered in hope. *If honorable men numbered Philip as their friend, then surely he was not as damnable as he was painted?*

Musing on this, she spent the day in the gallery looking at Philip's ancestors. When she tired of studying their aquiline noses and harsh countenance as captured by the deft hands of famous masters in oil paint, she ventured into the library and selected a title by Miss Austen. The day was spent idly reading the book that she borrowed. However, as the rain prevented her from venturing outside, even the escapades of Miss Elizabeth Bennet failed to keep her interest. Her mind kept wandering to her host and her own predicament: the dangers of staying at his home sans chaperone, and the feelings she was beginning to have for him.

She was relieved when the local doctor, a Dr. Carver, arrived and examined her coachman. He stopped at the library and, gratefully accepting the brandy preferred by Moseley, pronounced that Jim Coachman would be able to travel in a day or two. He did not advocate the long journey to Scotland, however.

Fiona knew that it was best to leave Crossfields and go away to Scotland and away from the disturbing presence of Lord Sheffield as she had planned. How would she manage it without Jim Coachman? She could not accept his lordship's offer to escort her to her relatives, nor could she stay his guest! What a fix! If all the rumors that circulated about him were true, how was her reputation going to survive this escapade? Was her virtue safe with a man of his repute? After all, cautious matrons had been known to shelter their daughters like mother hens when in the same gatherings which he attended. She had heard them whisper that no young girl was safe from his advances. Were those rumors to be heeded? He had behaved as a perfect gentleman to her. He had not so much as attempted to kiss her or hold her hand. *Not that I would have permitted it.* Nevertheless, he had not tried. *Could it be that he does not find me attractive?* She had thought to see a degree of admiration and even tenderness flit into his eyes the previous night, but it had quickly been replaced by his mask of boredom. She shook her head to stop herself from thinking such foolish thoughts. Whether he liked her or not was immaterial. He was a rake, and she a lady, and their paths should never have crossed. The sooner she forgot him the better. But no matter what she told herself, her errant mind insisted on contemplating the enigma that was Philip Merton. Oh! What was a girl to do?

Philip was likewise engaged in thinking of Fiona while in turn contemplating the fiasco that was his uninvited houseguest on his way to visit his friend. He was exhausted for having had little rest the night before. After drinking several glasses of brandy, he had finally taken himself off to bed, only to lie there tormented by images of her soft lips and guileless eyes. In the past when he had desired a woman, it had always been either a willing widow or an equally willing chorus girl. They had distracted him from his solitude but had left him feeling more alone when he finally ended the relationship with lavish gifts. Fiona was a vastly different article altogether. She was an innocent and well-bred lady. He could scarcely offer her a slip on the shoulder. If he knew her brother well, Ted would call him out for even entertaining such thoughts. So, in an effort to divert himself, he had decided to take up Cameron's invitation on impulse. Distance from her would certainly return him to his senses.

Sir Cameron's estate bordered Red Oaks, the country estate of Edward Cavendish, and it had taken Philip half a day to reach there. Cameron, a handsome man in a tall, big-boned way, with unruly hair and a somewhat-ruddy complexion, greeted him with every appearance of delight.

"Phil!" he had shouted, coming up to greet the horse and rider as Philip was dismounting. "You are a sight for sore eyes! It's been an age since I've clapped eyes on your ugly countenance! Where have you been hiding, old chap?" He interspersed his comments with several thumps across Philip's back.

Philip clasped his friend's proffered arm with a laugh. "Langton, trust you to bombard me with questions rather than offer a thirsty traveler a drink."

Cameron led the way to the house, which was part of a rambling country estate. Ensconced in the drawing room there, Philip encountered several friends and acquaintances that he hadn't seen in a while. Among them Lord Hector Bainbridge, Captain Colin Sanders otherwise known as "Sandy" to his friends, and Major Timothy Firth, who were all his schoolmates from Eton. Philip was well received by his peer group, despite his somewhat unsavory reputation. This was due in part to his own conduct, which was usually beyond reproach. He was known to be a great whip, a splendid rider, and handy with his fives. The latter the result of regular sessions at Gentleman Jacks Salon. All these traits allowed him to command no small degree of respect from the younger set. In addition, he was always polite if a little reserved and dressed in the best of taste, and his cravat tied in a simple waterfall was something that many a young man tried in vain to emulate. The gathering was well in their cups, though it was not yet midday, and they welcomed him with a rousing chorus of greetings and much back-thumping. Soon Philip was seated at the fireplace with the much-needed refreshment in hand, listening to stories from the war front as related by Major Firth and Captain Sanders.

"It was touch and go there for a while! What with the frogs attacking, and us being hard-pressed," Major Firth said, kneading his arm, which was encased in a sling. "Got hit by a shell fragment on the shoulder like a gudgeon. My men thought I was gone. If it weren't for Sandy here, I believe I might have been."

Sandy was a shy young man of few words. He offered a small smile, saying, "Tim's making much ado about nothing as usual. It was he who charged into the fray along with Ted Cavendish. I merely found him later half dead and pulled him to shelter."

The mention of Ted's name caught Philip's attention. He listened intently to learn more but was disappointed, for Firth continued the narrative saying, "I am lucky to be alive. We lost many good men that day. Carsten and Washington dead. Salisbury, Cheltenham, and Dorset injured, and many more are still unaccounted for."

"Is Cavendish thought to be alive?" Philip couldn't help asking.

The major, who was unaware of the history between the men, did not display any undue interest while responding. "Cavendish took a ball and went down. His batmen pulled him out of harm's way. When the fighting ended, we looked for them both but could find no trace. Just last week, we got wind that they are both still alive and that Ted is impatient to be discharged from the care of the old sawbones who has been treating him and wants to come home."

At this, Philip relapsed into silence as the news filled him with foreboding, and his mood turned pensive. The chatter of his friends flowed around him, but he did not join in. The conversation turned to sport and horses, and Lord Hector described the new Arabian he had acquired and ridden to the house party. This called for many exclamations of delight from the assembled men, and nothing would do but that he show them the new horse right then. Philip remained behind, claiming fatigue, while the men trooped out following Bainbridge, and quietude reigned in the drawing room. He was immersed in his own thoughts until his host came to find him a short while later.

"What ails you, old friend?" Langton asked in his direct way that none who knew him took offense with.

"Nothing really, just a bit of trouble due to the roads and the rains," Philip responded with a smile that did not touch his eyes.

"Don't you dare fob me off with gibberish about the weather, you old hand! Out with it! What's got you all in a twist?"

"If you must know, you interfering knucklehead, I am in somewhat of a pickle." Philip recounted the events of the past couple of days and the fact that Miss Cavendish now temporarily resided at his home. He ended his narrative, glumly saying, "Ted is not going to be amused when he finds his young sibling in the home of a notorious rake such as yours truly."

Cameron gave a hollow whistle. "What a ridiculous bumble broth! I don't see what else you could have done under the circumstance. Are the lady's faithful retainers close to mending? Is there any chance of them departing your premises before her brother descends on you breathing fire?"

"I wish I could say that they will be safely away, but my old sawbones, Carver, has declared that the coachman not be moved for a fortnight, and the chit refuses to leave without him."

"What do you intend to do, old chap? You can scarcely keep a gently born, unmarried female in a bachelor domicile."

"I don't want anything to do with her, much less keep her!" Philip exploded, his much put-upon temper erupting in protest.

"The way I see it, your goose is cooked no matter. If word gets out that she is under your protection, then you will have no choice but to offer for her. If her brother finds her at your place, he will surely call you out!" Cameron stated the obvious.

"I know that, but I don't see any way out of it. Be dammed if I offer for the chit. I don't even know her, let alone like her."

"Fat is she, then? Long in the tooth? Or dull-witted?" Cameron inquired artlessly.

"No, she is well-favored and better read than most females of my acquaintance. She can hold her own in a conversation too, and not just about gossip and fripperies but can speak at length about current affairs! She is also just out of the schoolroom and Ted's sister, to boot, so I will not be casting my card into the hat for her hand. Thank you very much," Philip reposited sternly, much to the amusement of his friend.

He brooded the rest of the day on the dilemma. In his mind, he listed all the elderly females among his relatives who might possibly be willing to come to him at a moment's notice. Given that he had rebuffed or antagonized most of them with his refusal to remarry and establish the family line, he doubted they would come even if he begged. However, he would try to appeal to his cousin Eliza, who was his favorite, and perhaps she would condescend to stay with him for a week and lend the whole situation an ounce of respectability. He had originally planned to spend a couple of days with his friends. He now decided to ride home at once to send off an invitation to Cousin Eliza. He also resolved to go himself to Fiona's uncle's residence and bring back someone who would talk some sense into her and escort her to Scotland forthwith. Either way, at the least he would have someone to act as a chaperone for the remainder of her stay.

A few hours later, after partaking of the entertainment and splendid repast provided by Cameron, he bade his friends goodbye. He did not offer any explanations to their surprised queries and made his early departure. He rode back home, using the long ride to cement his plans in his mind, and arriving in the early hours of the morning, took himself off to bed and fell asleep exhausted.

CHAPTER SEVEN

Ted's mood was black, and the musket wound on the right shoulder pained him, but he would not stop for rest. Anxiety as to the fate of his errant sister was making him feverish. He had been on the road for days. Stopping only to change teams and get food, he made it all the way to Gretna Green. At each stop, he had inquired about his sister, and he had learned that a lady matching her description had stopped at the Wandering Goose Inn. Hopeful at this, he had continued his journey only to discover that she had never made it to any of the next logical stops. Deducing that she had made run for Scotland, he had traveled day and night without finding any sign of his sister. Dejected, he retraced his steps but was obliged to detour on the return journey to avoid a mill that was in progress in Chillingham, and thus found himself in the village of Catton. Having been on the road for the better part of two days, he was very tired, and following the advice of Bates, he decided to spend the night at the Bear and Knight, the only local hostelry.

The host, seeing his raiment and carriage, recognized quality and gave them his best rooms. Cavendish soon washed and changed, and suddenly feeling ravenous, made his way to the taproom with Bates, hoping to get some vittles. There the host seated them close to the fire, and he ordered a hearty meal and a large tankard. Taking a healthy swig of his ale, Ted contemplated on his next course of action. There seemed nothing for it but to return to London and ask for help from Bow Street. His thirst satisfied, his keen eyes took in his surroundings and the other occupants of the taproom.

There was an old farm hand snoring over his half-empty tankard and several tradesmen enjoying a good meal. Gathered around the fire were a few soldiers back from the war. He decided that he would make inquiries of the host about his sister once he was done with his meal. Turning back to Bates, he told him that they would continue their search the following day. Just then the taproom door opened, and a rough-looking man walked in. He was hailed by several of the other occupants.

"Come 'n' sit with us, Higgins," one of the assembled men called. "What news?"

The newcomer walked over to the table from where he had been addressed and sat down and called for drink. He looked around at his expectant audience in the manner of one who has a tale worth telling. "You'll and believe the goings-on at that place," he said.

"You know I work at Sir Graham's farm whenever he needs an extra helping hand, and his land runs close to the Crossfields estate farms. Well, there I was this past day and heard the strangest bit o' noos." He paused for effect and took a swig of his ale.

Edward looked up in surprise at mention of Crossfields, his interest aroused in spite of himself. He turned to look at the speaker and listened to the ensuing conversation.

"Go on then, what's his lor'ship been up to now? Brung his doxies home for one of them orgeez that I heard happen in Lunnon town among the quality?" asked one of his audience hopefully.

"He brung a female there all right, only this one ain't be a doxy. Rumor be that he has kidnapped a young girl and is keeping her there against her will." He paused again in satisfaction at the audible gasp his revelation caused. At the next table, Edward sat up in attention, a nasty suspicion beginning to take shape in his mind.

"Higgins, are ye pulling a fast one on us, then? Even Sheffield wouldn't do somethin' so depraved as to kidnap a young girl," the fascinated audience protested.

"But he did so, and she be a girl of quality too. She was traveling in her own coach with an abygel no less, and I heard as Sheffield stops the coach and shot the coachman and made off with the girl and the abygel. Quality! Pah! No beter'n a highwayman that one!" he spat. "It were two days ago, it were, and no one seen 'em since. The farmhands say as he's keepin' her pris'ner and forcin' her to do his biddin', if you get my drift." Higgins leered and gave a big wink.

Edward did not wait to hear more. Forgetting the meal he had ordered, he rushed out of the taproom and hollered for Bates to get their carriage ready. Running up to their rooms, he returned with his pistols. In a matter of minutes, they were speeding up the highway on their way to Crossfields.

Consumed by a blazing rage, he swore vengeance on Sheffield. How dare Sheffield lure his innocent sister to his den of vice. What kind of libertine would seduce a helpless girl? *If Sheffield has dared to lay so much as a finger on Fiona, I will have his heart out,* Edward swore under his breath as he set a furious pace to Sheffield's home, enduring the discomfort of the rutted road in grim silence, planning to heap all kinds of horrible punishments on Sheffield's head.

CHAPTER EIGHT

Fiona woke up late the following day after another restless night. It had been four days since she left home, and her mind was in turmoil about what she should do. If she went back to her brother's house in London, her cousin Sadie could well force her into marriage to Harry. Continuing on to Scotland while Jim Coachman was still so poorly, could not be considered.

She was well aware that her presence in Sheffield's home made him uneasy. Her feelings toward him were also disturbing. She was aware that her opinion of her host had undergone a subtle change. Far from thinking him the villain of the piece, she was inclined to cast him as a tragic and misunderstood hero. That would never do! Villain or hero, whatever he may be, but she could not stay indefinitely in his house in any case. If anyone knew she had stayed at his home sans chaperone for so many days, she would be well and truly compromised. Though Philip had conducted himself with honor, his past would tear them both with impropriety. Philip may feel honor-bound to offer for her, or worse, Ted would call Philip out! The very thought was thoroughly depressing. Feeling cooped up in the great estate and desperately needing some exercise, she thought to go for a ride. It would clear her head off the cobwebs, and she may yet come up with a way to get out of the mess she had landed in.

She breakfasted in her room, and with Marcie's help, donned her green riding habit and matching hat. It was close to noon when she made her way downstairs. She thought to see Philip and request a horse and even nursed a faint hope that he may offer to accompany her. Her hopes were dashed when she was informed by Moseley that the master had left to inspect some rain damage at the home farm. Hiding her disappointment, she asked Moseley to request that the grooms saddle a horse for her and asked if the cook could be troubled to make her a sandwich to take with her. Moseley gave a dubious look and mumbled something about waiting for the master, as most of the grooms had been called to assist in the repairs.

"Please, Moseley," she beseeched him prettily. "My head is all fuddled, and I really could use some fresh, country air. Just look at the beautiful day. Wouldn't it be grand to eat in the fresh air on a day like this? If we waited for Lord Sheffield, the sunlight could well be gone. It may well rain again on the morrow."

Moseley, unable to resist her appeal, acquiesced. She went down to the stables and found that the stable boy had saddled a gentle mare for her. A footman fetched a bag with some food and placed it inside the saddlebags. Fiona mounted the mare and was pleasantly surprised to find her to be a goer.

Craving solitude, she refused the grooms' offer to accompany her. She set off at brisk pace, savoring the afternoon sunlight and the fresh air. She rode in the direction that she assumed was toward the home farm. The fresh air and exercise soon revived her. She urged the mare to a canter and then to a gallop, exhilarating in the feelings of the powerful hooves thundering on the ground and of the wind in her hair. They encountered a narrow stream, which she gracefully jumped over, landing safely on the other side laughing out loud, her woes forgotten in the thrill of the moment.

She found a little thicket on the other side, and there she dismounted and let the horse graze. She spied a patch of daisies and gathered a few flowers to make into a chain, as she used to do in her childhood at Red Oaks before Mama and Papa had died. Soon she became aware that she was not alone. A little, brown mongrel with half-bent ears and a plume of a tail was sitting not far from her, its bright eyes intent on her hands. Fond of dogs and well versed in their ways, she acted as if she had not seen him, hoping to coax him nearer. Her trick worked. Soon a little, wet muzzle was sniffing at her. She stretched out her hand to the puppy, for that's what it was, then gently scratched its ears. The puppy gave her hand a big, slobbery lick.

Searching in the saddlebags, she took out the cold chicken sandwich, apple, and bottle of lemonade she found there. She broke off a piece of the sandwich and fed it to the puppy, watching in delight as he wolfed it down. Another piece followed, and soon the sandwich was gone. Fiona contented herself with the apple and the lemonade. "What shall I call you?" Fiona asked the mutt.

"Woof!" the puppy responded.

"So be it," Fiona laughed. "Wolfie."

The day had grown warm, and feeling drowsy, she sat down with her back to a tree, thinking to rest a bit before returning. The mongrel settled at her feet with his head on her boot. The sunlight filtered through the leaves and fell on her. The day was shrouded in peace and tranquility. Fiona let the quietude calm her apprehensions about her situation, and soon the warmth of the afternoon lulled her to sleep.

⋖————◆————⋗

Philip was not having a quiet day by any means. After barely a couple of hours of rest, he was roused by his valet, Samuels, to be informed that his bailiff had called with urgent business to be discussed. Still weary from his journey of the previous night, he had roused himself reluctantly. It was barely seven o'clock when he gulped the hot coffee that Samuels brought to him and washed and dressed and headed to his study where his bailiff, Masters, was waiting for him.

Masters brought him news that the recent storm had caused considerable damage in the home farm. He explained that he had come to see Philip the previous day, but that Philip had been away from home. He said that it was imperative Philip visited the tenants and inspect the damage for himself. They would need to discuss the repairs and decide whether to hire help to carry them out. Philip cursed his luck. He had hoped to leave for Scotland to investigate Fiona's relations, but he would now have to postpone that trip until the next day. His tenants' problem required his immediate attention. He had his horse saddled and accompanied Masters to the home farm.

Philip spent the rest of the afternoon reassuring the tenants and taking inventory of the damage to the various houses. He then organized the farmhands and grooms into groups and assigned them to conduct the repairs. He himself dressed down to his shirtsleeves and worked with Masters fencing a pasture on higher ground for the cattle. They worked the whole day, stopping briefly to lunch on the food that Mrs. Pork sent out to them. A mist set in late in the afternoon and forced the men to stop working. Philip dispensed the grooms, but he remained with Masters to inspect the repairs to the roofs and speak with the tenant farmer about the care of the animals. It was almost dusk when he finally returned home with Masters, intending to discuss the next day's plans with him.

Moseley met them at the door with a troubled expression on his face.

"What is it, Moseley, not more bad news surely?" Philip asked, concerned.

"It's Miss Fiona, your lordship," Moseley said, looking very uncomfortable. "She went riding late this morning and has not yet returned."

"She rode out alone?"

"Yes, your lordship, and her horse had come back riderless and muddied about the fetlocks. I fear she may have taken a tumble." Moseley looked genuinely distressed. "As the grooms were all occupied, I set a couple of footmen to look for her, and they haven't returned yet."

Philip went cold with dread when he heard that she had been gone for several hours. His first thought was that she had been thrown and was lying dying in a ditch. That thought propelled him into action. He first gave Moseley a stern set down for not sending word to him earlier. He then went and spoke to the grooms and was informed that the riderless mare had returned over an hour earlier. He told the head groom to saddle up the horses and to assemble all the available stable hands and grooms for a search party. The men, though tired from the long day of hard labor, complied without complaint, as they knew he was just as tired from working alongside them.

"Light several lanterns. And get the maid Elsie to bring something of hers so we can set the hounds on her scent." He stopped, feeling a large raindrop on his head. The next minute, his shirtsleeves were soaked. Cursing, he ran to the house for his greatcoat when Mrs. Pork accosted him, twisting her apron in her hands and looking fearful.

"If it pleases your lordship, I must speak to you," she said in an imploring voice.

"Surely it can wait, Mrs. Pork. Time is of the essence if we are to have any chance of finding Miss Cavendish in this mist. If she has taken a tumble in the rain, she may be unconscious and hurt. The dratted rain is going to make it harder to find her."

He started to turn away, but Mrs. Pork stayed him, saying, "I'm afraid that Miss Cavendish may have run away again, your lordship."

Philip stopped short and rounded on her. "What do you mean 'again'?" he demanded.

"Well, my lord, that day when the bee stung, she was distraught and confided in me. She said that she was running away from home to Scotland to avoid getting married to a gentleman that her family had chosen. I should have perhaps informed you earlier, but I did not want to break her confidence." Mrs. Pork sounded tremulous as she confessed her omission.

Though he was truly alarmed by this information, Philip managed to remain outwardly calm. He reassured Mrs. Pork that, though it certainly would have helped to know earlier, she had done the right thing in telling him now. He then ran back to the stable, mounted his horse, and rode out in a gallop followed by the grooms. Not knowing the direction Fiona had taken, he split up the men and sent them to search the different parts of the estate. He kept two grooms and the hounds with him and rode in the direction that the grooms said her mare had returned from.

Riding like a madman, calling out her name, all the while fearing the worst, Philip was at his wit's end. Mrs. Pork's confession had put a new twist on things. The situation had just taken a definite turn for the worse. Not only had he brought an unchaperoned young lady to his house, but she had run away from home. Her family had probably been searching for her while he had blithely believed her story and allowed her to remain in his house. The ton would have a field day with this. They would blame him, as he richly deserved, for not informing her family immediately after the accident as he should have. Fiona would be ruined. *Fiona!* He cursed in frustration. She had just made matters infinitely worse for both of them by leaving his home unescorted. It was quite probable that she had understood his intent of contacting her relatives and run away again. He had to find her! Then it slowly dawned on him that it was logical that if Fiona had run away from home and headed toward Scotland, she may have been eloping to meet a lover at Gretna Green. This thought caused him such an intense wave of rage that he involuntarily spurred his horse mercilessly onward. It was only when his grooms, who had galloped to catch up with him, looked at him questioningly that he realized what he was doing and stopped spurring and apologized to his mount. As they rode on, his anger was swiftly replaced by an overwhelming concern and anxiety for Fiona's safety.

———◇———

Fiona woke with a start and found that the sun had set while she slept. Quickly rising, she brushed her skirt and looked for her mare but couldn't find it. Guessing that it must have wandered back home, she mentally cursed her luck and started walking briskly in the direction of the house. The sky was hidden by ominous clouds, but there was still light, and she made good progress for a while. She soon reached the stream she had crossed earlier and looking for a bridge to cross did not find one. She had no choice but to hoist the skirts of her habit and wade through the cold water. She had almost made it across when her riding boot slipped on a smooth stone, and she fell. Thoroughly wet, she cursed freely as she clambered up the farther bank. She wrung out her habit and then discovered that she had lost her hat in the stream, and her hair was hanging down around her face in wet disarray. Close to tears, she started walking again, hoping to reach the house before nightfall.

A thick mist quickly set in and engulfed her, so she was no longer sure if she was going in the right direction. It dawned on her that in galloping her horse she had ridden farther than she realized and now knew not where she was. Her soaked riding boots hurt her feet, and soon she started feeling fatigued and slowed down. A rumble in her belly reminded her that she had eaten nothing but an apple since breakfast, and that had been several hours ago. Her body was reminding her in no uncertain terms that it needed nourishment.

Tears made tracks on her dusty cheeks, flowing unheeded as the hopelessness of the situation overcame her. A small yelp near her feet made her look down. She saw that Wolfie was looking up at her, wagging his tail. He yelped and ran ahead. "Clever boy! Do you know the way, then?" she called, hurrying to follow the puppy.

Just when she thought it couldn't get worse, the sky darkened, and rain set in. She kept walking, hoping that she was still going in the right direction. It became very dark soon, and she could barely see a few feet ahead. She feared that she would have to stay out all night. In her tired, wet state, the shadows around her seemed more ominous; familiar shapes of trees appeared eerie, shrouded in the mist. It seemed to her that she had been walking for hours, and she was close to exhaustion when she finally heard the sound of hounds barking in the distance. Wolfie let out a series of answering yelps. Soon, to her relief, she heard the hoofbeats of an approaching rider.

"I'm here," she called out. "Help! Please!" Her voice sounded small and tremulous. *Will it even penetrate the mist? Will the rider hear me?* Wolfie continued yelping and prancing about in excitement. The hoofbeats grew increasingly louder, and she saw the glimmer of a lantern. The dark figure of a rider galloped in breathtaking speed to rein up in front of her. She had never been gladder to see anyone in her life as she recognized Philip.

Relief that Fiona was safe was the overwhelming emotion Philip felt when he saw her. That emotion was swiftly replaced by a surge of anger at her for giving them cause for worry. He jumped off the saddle even before his horse stopped and ran to her, gripping her by the shoulders and scanning her face furiously once there.

"Fiona! Are you all right?" he shouted, using her given name as if it were the most natural thing, in his anxious state. He could feel Fiona shivering in his grasp as she nodded.

Two more lanterns approached as the grooms rode up just then. Philip was torn between wanting to hug her in relief, to quiz her, to make sure and reassure himself that she was unhurt, and to shake her for wandering off and worrying them all to death. However, minding the presence of the grooms, he restrained himself and did none of these things. He saw that her gown was soaked and that she was dripping wet and shivering with cold. Without a word, he peeled off his overcoat and draped it over her. Then, without so much as a by your leave, he picked her up as if she were a rag sack and deposited her on his horse.

He nodded to the grooms to follow and, mounting behind her, galloped away.

"Wait!" Fiona cried, tugging at his shirt and pointing. He looked with a frown at what she was pointing to and saw a puppy that looked like a drowning rat. It was wagging its tail and prancing about the hooves of his horse. He looked at Fiona.

"Please! Wolfie saved me. He led me to you," she said, looking at him beseechingly. At that moment, he couldn't have denied her anything. Dismounting, he scooped up the little puppy and handed him to a groom. The puppy was soon safely ensconced inside the groom's coat and out of the rain, and the tired procession of puppy, grooms, and hounds followed Philip home.

Philip, feeling Fiona shivering against him, set off at a furious speed in the direction he had come. The two grooms followed at a respectable distance. The ride home was quiet. He remained silent, not trusting himself to speak politely, and he could sense that she was too tired to talk. Resting against his chest and in the comfort of his arms, he felt that she was a part of himself that had been missing for a long time that he had now reclaimed.

Once home, one of the grooms ran up to them and reached up for her, and Philip handed her over to him gently and dismounted. He then took her from the groom and carried her into the house himself. Still half-asleep, Fiona protested feebly that she could walk, but he did not seem to hear her. Mrs. Pork, Moseley, Elsie, and Marcie came running to meet them with cries of relief, but he did not stop for them. He marched up the stairs purposefully until he reached her room. A footman ran to throw open the door, and he strode in and deposited her unceremoniously on the bed.

Fully awake now, Fiona sat up and tried to thank Philip, but he was gone before she could speak, closing the door behind him. She limped to the mirror and was appalled at her forlorn appearance. Mud streaked her face, her habit was splattered and soaking wet, and her hair hung around her face and shoulders in ratty, sopping, and unkempt coils. Fiona was too worn out to do more than creep back to bed and lay down. Feeling cold, she pulled his coat that she had let fall on the bed close around her and let a few tears of self-pity trickle down her cheeks unheeded.

She was not allowed to wallow for long. Mrs. Pork and Marcie soon came bustling in with hot water and a tea tray. A hip bath was set up in front of the fire, and she was stripped of her wet clothes and made to sit in it while Marcie fussed over her and related how anxious the household had been.

"You gave us such a turn, miss. I was that scared that you had gone and left me behind or fallen off the horse and been killed." She sniffed as she washed out the mud from Fiona's hair. "I was that scared when I heard that your horse came back without you."

"The master was beside himself with worry," Mrs. Pork said kindly as she handed Fiona a cup of tea. All Fiona remembered was the flash of anger she had seen in Philip's eyes. Even during the ride home, though she had felt secure in his arms, she had sensed the anger emanating from him. She allowed herself to dwell on how secure she had felt to snuggle in the depths of his coat, warmed by his body. She had drifted off to sleep in weariness by the time they reached the stables. *Had he really been concerned or am I a mere inconvenience?*

Mrs. Pork inquired whether she would want a tray to be sent up instead of going down for dinner. "I will have dinner sent up, my lady, you get a good night's rest. You will feel much better in the morning," Mrs. Pork encouraged.

Fiona was strongly tempted to put off meeting with her host until the next day but determined not to be cowed by him. "I am much restored, Mrs. Pork. If it's all the same, I will come downstairs. Please let Lord Sheffield know that I am fine and will be downstairs shortly."

Mrs. Pork then left, saying kindly that she would ask dinner to be set back by an hour.

Marcie dried Fiona's hair by the fire and dressed it into a simple style. She then helped Fiona get dressed. Fiona chose her favorite gown to give herself some confidence. The beautiful, rich, rose color offset her wan complexion, which even the warm bath had failed to restore.

"You look pretty, miss," Marcie said, admiring her own handiwork when she was done. Glancing at herself in the mirror, Fiona did not see the pretty girl in the beautiful gown. Instead, she saw herself as a lamb going to the slaughter. Summoning all her courage, she went downstairs, determined to face the lion in his den.

Moseley met her at the foot of the stairs and told her that the master awaited her in his study.

I am properly in for it now, Fiona thought, but resolving not to feel intimidated, she steeled herself for the confrontation and made her way slowly to the study. Her knock received a curt response to enter, and she walked in and closed the door behind her. In the short time that she had known Philip, she could read his mood. He was upset about something; she could tell from his voice. Was it because of her stupidity in getting lost? Whatever it was that was on his mind, she sensed she was going to get a dressing down and preferred that the servants not hear the set down she was sure to receive.

Philip was standing near the fireplace, leaning against the mantelpiece, a large glass of brandy in his hand. He had changed out of his wet clothes and was dressed for dinner. There was no sign of anger in his face as he turned toward her. Instead, it held his customary expression of boredom, and he looked, if possible, even more cynical than usual.

"Miss Cavendish, it is extremely good of you to make an appearance," he drawled when he saw her.

"I am sorry if I kept you waiting, my lord," Fiona said defensively, marching up to stand in front of him and look at him bravely.

He did not ask her to be seated but instead said with a cynical smile, "Is that all you are sorry about?"

"Beg your pardon, my lord. I—" Fiona started to apologize but was rudely interrupted by her host.

"Miss Cavendish, since your arrival, you have turned my household upside down. My staff has been stretched thin caring for your coachman and abigail. You have flouted every rule in this house. But today you have also displayed a remarkable lack of consideration for everyone here. Not only have I had to reprimand Moseley for not informing me of your departure but also have had to reprimand my stable hand for letting you ride off without an escort. You have also caused Mrs. Pork and the maids unnecessary distress when you did not return from your ride this afternoon. In addition, my men, who were already weary from a hard day's work, had to scour the countryside looking for you in the rain. There is no doubt that several of them will take to bed with colds on the morrow when I have urgent need of hands to make repairs to the damage caused by the storm. I hope you are satisfied."

His words made Fiona feel like she was ten inches tall. Her tender heart sank as she realized that so many people had been inconvenienced by her. Truly remorseful, she lowered her eyes in contrition. "I am sorry to have caused you so much trouble, my lord," she mumbled. "I meant no harm. I just went for a ride and had the misfortune to fall asleep. The mare wandered off, and I got lost in the mist and couldn't find my way back."

"A situation which could have been avoided if you had let me know of your intention of going for a ride." Philip's voice was cold and dispassionate. "I would have warned you about the mist that can creep up on you when it rains around here. If you had accepted an escort of a groom, then you would not have been lost, as my grooms know the estate well enough to ride about blindfolded. Instead, your stubborn and impetuous nature has caused distress to my household and could have landed you in real harm. It is by luck that you were found unharmed."

Fiona felt like a naughty child being reprimanded after being caught red-handed in an act of mischief. "I truly regret the inconvenience I have caused you, my lord. If I could have avoided it, I would have!" she cried, her temper flaring and her eyes flashing like sparklers.

Philip did not seem to notice her emotional state. "Would you, Miss Cavendish?" he continued relentlessly. "I am not sure I believe that. You are a spoiled, hoydenish creature who can only think of herself. Else why would you have failed to tell me the complete truth earlier when you had every opportunity? Knowing full well the differences that exist between your brother and me, you never once mentioned that you had run away from home. You deceived me from the start to remain here under false pretenses. Do you realize that you have placed me in an incredibly difficult position?"

Fiona tensed and glanced up at him as she realized that her deception had been found out. She hung her head in apprehension.

Philip continued mercilessly, "tell me, Miss Cavendish, do you really have an uncle in Scotland, or is that a fabrication too? Perhaps it is not a relative that you were on your way to meet, but a lover?" he asked silkily.

Outrage made Fiona see red. How dare he imply that she was eloping to meet clandestinely with a lover? Her head held high, eyes flashing, she turned on him in rage.

"Whom I go to meet is none of your concern, my lord," she cried. "I have already apologized for inconveniencing you. What more do you want from me?"

"I want you gone from here," he barked. "You shouldn't be here without a chaperone in the first place. If word gets out, you will be properly compromised. Or is that your intent all along? To trap me in the parson's mousetrap?"

Fiona gasped at his rudeness.

"What a fickle woman you must think me that I should leave home for one lover and change my mind and try to trap another in a matter of days," she cried. Her eyes smarted with tears of anger. "Surely you flatter yourself, my lord. I would rather wed a slimy worm than wed a rake and libertine such as you."

"Your erratic behavior speaks for itself, Miss Cavendish. I merely interpret it as I see fit," Philip responded, examining his fingernails with the air of extreme boredom.

Fiona had taken all the insults she could handle for one night. How dare a rake, and one with a reputation like his, no less, criticize and judge her. She walked up to him, her very being emanating fury, and slapped him on his face. Still unappeased, she raised her hand again, but it was caught in an iron grip. Seizing her by her arms, Philip pulled her toward him and held her roughly against his chest with one hand and caught her chin with his other. She struggled futilely against him and beat on his chest with her free hand but to no avail. Staring into her enraged eyes, he smiled aggravatingly.

"Do you know what happens to little girls who play with fire, Miss Cavendish? You know my reputation well, yet here you are alone and helpless. How tempting for a libertine of my repute?" he purred.

She stilled in his arms, mesmerized by the fire in his eyes, knowing through some feminine instinct that she was about to be kissed. He held her chin firmly and lowered his head toward hers. Fiona was motionless, frozen as his lips drew closer. His mouth descended on hers in a punishing kiss. She experienced an onslaught of sensation that set her body on fire. Closing her eyes, she succumbed to his kiss. The kiss turned into one of surprising tenderness. For a moment, she forgot her anger and lost herself in his embrace. She kissed him back, not wanting him to stop.

Philip held her close, and that kiss touched Fiona all the way into her, heartwarming her and making her toes curl. She responded with endearing innocence, feeling her own passion kindling to a flame. He awoke sensations no man had done before. Her innocence awakened a curiosity that was an enticement to experience all the pleasure that being in his arms promised. And she kissed him as if he couldn't give her enough. She felt the kiss deepen, and heat coursed through her as her whole body tingled with awareness. Desire sparked into flame, and she threw her arms around his neck with abandon, twining her fingers through his luxurious hair.

She felt him withdraw as he relinquished her lips slowly, and he looked down at her with a bemused expression. His eyes, a mere breath away from hers, looked brooding and strangely vulnerable. She gazed back at him in confusion with eyes that were still wet with unshed tears. His arms still held her close, and in that moment of silence, she could hear his heart thudding close to her own breast, as if they both beat with the same rhythm. They remained thus for a moment, looking into each other's eyes, and neither heard the sound of raised voices and the commotion that was ensuing outside.

The door suddenly burst open, and they both started. Philip released her immediately, and she sprang away just as Colonel Ted Cavendish burst into the room like a hurricane.

CHAPTER NINE

Edward, tired and famished with hunger, came crashing through Philip's study, and the first thing he saw was Fiona in tears, clasped in Philip's arms, and his temper knew no bounds. With a cry of outrage, he advanced on Philip and dealt him a blow to his jaw that knocked him down.

"Sheffield!" he cried, enraged. "Take your filthy hands off my sister, you cad! You will meet me for that."

Fiona ran into his arms and hugged him. "Oh! Ted, you are back safe! Oh, thank heavens! How glad I am to see you. I have been sick with worry." Then seeing his arm in a sling, she cried in concern, "Oh! My dearest! Are you badly hurt?"

"Fiona, dearest girl, what a fine chase you have led me. I am fine and almost recovered. But enough about me. Tell me, are you all right? Has this vile creature assaulted you or harmed you in any way?"

Blushing crimson, Fiona shook her head and buried her face in her brother's shoulder.

"Thank God for small mercies! I came just in time, then."

"Amen to that." They both turned toward Philip, who was back on his feet and watching this emotional reunion with his usual bored cynicism. "Cavendish, please take your sister away from here and leave me in peace."

"Not so fast, Sheffield. Not before you tell me why she is here in the first place," Edward barked. "Rumor has it that you shot her coachman and kidnapped her."

"And is that what you believe?" Philip's voice was dangerously quiet.

"No! Ted, that's not true," Fiona intervened hurriedly. "Our carriage had an accident near here, and Jim Coachman and Marcie were both hurt. I would have been stranded if Lord Sheffield had not happened to be traveling by at that time. He and his men rescued us and brought us here. That was almost four days ago. Jim Coachman's leg is broken, and Marcie has injuries as well, and I couldn't leave without them. Lord Sheffield has been exceedingly kind and let me stay here, and I am truly indebted to him."

"It seems that he has already been reclaiming some of that debt in his own abhorrent way." Ted's voice dripped with contempt. "If the scene I interrupted was anything to go by, he was taking advantage of your helplessness to force his unwanted attentions on you."

Fiona blushed in confusion and tongue-tied, was unable to offer her brother an explanation. Philip merely shrugged and said nothing.

Impatient, Ted turned to leave. "My carriage will arrive shortly to collect my sister's belongings and our servants. You may ask your seconds to call on me at my country estate. That is if you can find anyone to second you." With that parting shot, Edward turned on his heel and stalked in hauteur from the room. Her heart feeling like it was plummeting slowly to lodge between her toes, Fiona cast a despairing look at Philip. Their gazes held, and in that brief moment, she glimpsed an unfathomable emotion in his eyes . . . what was it? Anguish? Despair? Regret? Before she could decipher, it was gone, replaced by a cynical sneer. Philip made an exaggerated bow, and Fiona turned away to hide her confusion and the hurt that almost made her steps falter as she hurried after her brother, tears smarting and lips trembling as she struggled to rein in the turbulent emotions that stormed in her breast.

Philip remained standing, staring at the fire for some time. He then turned and walked to the brandy decanter and poured himself a large glass. He suddenly felt drained and hollow, as if Fiona in leaving had taken a piece of his being with her. His mind dwelled on Fiona; how divine it had felt to hold her in his arms! Their kiss had been an eye-opener. It had beguiled him and ignited feelings that he had not experienced in years. And even while he had submitted to his own need to feel alive, he had recognized that she was an innocent, inexperienced and naïve. Cavendish was right, he had arrived just in time. "A rake and libertine!" Her words echoed in his ears. The epithets she had flung at him had been sharp and true and found their mark. His ego bruised and hurting, he had reacted in anger, acting abominably and proving her right. There was no excuse for his behavior, and he would accept his punishment at Ted's hands in the duel. In fact, he welcomed it; Ted could only hurt his body and perhaps claim his life. Fiona had already exacted a far greater price. She had penetrated his heart. In one gulp, he finished his drink and then flung the glass into the fire, angry at himself.

CHAPTER TEN

Fiona was a very troubled young lady in the days that followed. She and Ted had returned to their country home, Red Oaks. Edward, true to his word, had dispatched a carriage to bring Marcie and Jim Coachman and their belongings home. The butler, Sudbury, and part of the household staff had joined them at Red Oaks, leaving Cousin Sadie and Harry to fend for themselves in London. By all counts, she should have been happy. However, the toll of the past few days had caught up with the inveterate soldier, and Ted had collapsed out of exhaustion. The exertion of the tiring journey and the extreme stress he had put upon himself caused his injury to worsen, and he had to be confined to his bed. He soon developed a fever. Apprehensive, Fiona had summoned their physician. That good gentleman examined Ted and pronounced that his wound had become inflamed and that his body was very weak. He said that if he did not rest for the next few days, infection would set in, and then his chances of recovery would be slim.

An anxious Fiona followed his directions faithfully and kept her brother confined to his bed for the next few days. By the end of the third day, the fever was gone, and Edward was restless to be up. On the morning of the fourth day, they received a visit from Lord Hector Bainbridge and Sir Cameron Langton. Fiona greeted them with nervous trepidation, oblivious to the admiring glances they sent her way. Nothing would stop Ted from going down to meet them. He knew them well as old class fellows from Eton, but they had come there on that day representing Philip Merton on the matter of the duel. Fiona, who was excluded from the conversation of the three men, unashamedly eavesdropped at the door of the study and heard enough to know that the date for the duel was set for two days hence. Aghast that her brother, who had just recovered, would even contemplate fighting a duel in his weakened state, she resolved that she would do all in her might to prevent it. She denied to herself that part of her resolve was also out of concern for Philip.

When Lord Bainbridge and Sir Langton had taken their leave, Fiona cornered Ted in his study. Hoping to avert the duel, she confessed to her brother the details of her adventures: her cousin Sadie's scheme to announce her engagement to Harry Albrighton in his absence, her flight to Scotland, and how she had stayed at Sheffield's house because she had not dared to go back to her cousin.

Ted listened to her without interrupting, except for the occasional exclamation at parts of her narrative. When she finished, she peeped up at him to judge his reaction.

"Are you terribly angry with me, dearest? Have I made a mull of things?"

"You have been very naughty, little one, but I forgive you, as it is partly my fault for having left you to Cousin Sadie's tender mercies. But you must never behave in such hoydenish fashion again. You were lucky that Philip Merton did not take advantage of you." He gave her a reassuring hug.

"But, Ted, don't you see?" Fiona persisted. "I had no choice but to flee. Cousin Harry was pressing me to wed or threatened to cut me off without a penny. As you know, I must be wed by the age of twenty-one or forfeit my inheritance."

"I am aware of that, and I had hoped that you would have a formal debut by now and be surrounded by adoring suitors and have your pick of offers."

"I did, dear brother. I had plenty of both."

"But none that you liked, eh, chick?"

"None that touched my heart, brother dear, and I have no inclination to marry without love."

"Oh! Chick, there are still a few weeks till your birthday, and now that I am home, we will attend all the festivities. There is bound to be some young dandy or nonpareil who will catch your fancy. Never you fear."

His words conjured up a cynical face with deep pools for eyes, and her fears came rushing back into her heart.

"Only if you survive this duel, Ted. If anything were to happen to you, I may as well die too," Fiona cried, tears glistening in her green eyes and spilling onto her cheeks. "Can you not call it off? For my sake, dearest brother?"

Seeing Ted's jaw assuming a familiar stubborn set, she rushed into more pleas before he could speak.

"Philip . . . I mean, Lord Sheffield behaved as a true gentleman. It was my fault that you found us in such a compromising state. He was unduly provoked that day. Surely it is unjust to blame him entirely."

"Was it also your fault that you had tears in your eyes, then?" Ted demanded wrathfully. Fiona did not have any response to that. "You lie to avert this duel. I know what I saw, and that scoundrel has abused an innocent girl for the last time. This time I will make him pay a price that he will not soon forget."

She wept and pleaded with him to reconsider. She said that he had just returned to her and that he was cruel to put himself in danger again. Her tears had no effect on her brother. He bluntly refused to even discuss the duel anymore. He said it was a matter of honor and that she should cease to interfere in it. When she further protested that his health was too weak and that he should at least consider setting it for a later date, he had gently ushered her from the study saying that he had to catch up with his affairs and that she shouldn't worry her pretty head about it.

Fiona was annoyed at once again being treated like a child, and this time by her own brother. She cursed the pigheadedness of the male species. Yet she would not let the matter rest. Fraught with worry, she decided that if Ted would not listen to reason, she would try his adversary instead.

The next day, taking advantage of her brother's visit to London to meet with his man of business, Fiona set out for Crossfields. She dressed with care in a new gown of pale-green silk and a matching pelisse lined with ermine. A bonnet trimmed with green ribbons set off her chestnut locks to perfection, with a few becoming tendrils artlessly framing her face. Twisting and turning at her mirror, she looked fetching, but if she were to win this round, she needed to use all the ammunition she could muster. Summoning a footman, she instructed him to ready the gig. Desiring privacy, she did not allow Marcie to accompany her, saying she was going for a drive to clear her head. The entire drive was spent imagining his reaction to the proposition she had in mind. By the time she reached Crossfields in the late afternoon, she had worked herself into an extremely nervous state.

When Moseley opened the door to her, he looked at her in surprise. "Hello, Moseley, is his lordship in?" Fiona said with a reassuring smile and sailed right in. Moseley followed her, saying that Lord Sheffield was in his study and had asked not to be disturbed. Before he could stop her, she moved past him and toward the study.

She approached the door with trepidation, steeling herself with a reminder that she had no choice but to try. There were two lives at stake if she failed. She had to save her brother and Philip at all costs. It was too late to turn back now, at all events.

Fiona opened the door without knocking and was about to enter when a small bark startled her. Looking around, she saw Wolfie gamboling toward her, yapping and wagging his tail. The sight of him heartened her and gave her confidence, and she bent down to scratch his ears as he bounced up and down in a vain effort to lick her face.

Philip looked up from behind the desk and shot to his feet in apparent astonishment. "Down, Wolfie!" he called, and Wolfie obediently returned to him, tail wagging and tongue lolling. She marveled at the changed appearance of her canine friend. He looked well cared for and much improved and much attached to his new master. The affection was mutual, she suspected.

"Miss Cavendish," Philip said, bowing politely. Could it be admiration she glimpsed in his eyes before he schooled them to his usual façade of amused boredom? "To what do I owe this unexpected pleasure?"

Just the sight of him was causing her insides to flip, and she was sorely tempted to flee; however, his obvious kindness in adopting the mongrel lent her courage. "Lord Sheffield, I need to talk to you on a matter of some urgency." Fiona's voice sounded uncertain to her own ears.

Leading her to a chair near the fireplace, he waited for her to be seated before seating himself. She refused his offer of refreshment, and not knowing how to begin, she sat with her face lowered and twisted her reticule restlessly on her lap.

A long moment of silence passed until Philip leaned forward to ask gently, "Something ails you as I can see. How may I be of assistance?"

She looked up at him then and was surprised to see a look of tenderness flit briefly into his eyes. She blinked, and when she looked again, he was studying his manicured fingernails with rapt attention. Taking her courage in her hands, she dived right in.

"Philip, I need your help," she started nervously. If he was startled at her use of his given name, he did not demur, and encouraged by this, she continued. "I must ask you not to fight my brother tomorrow."

She heard him swearing softly under his breath as he drew himself up to his full height and towered above her with alarming disapproval. "I am afraid I cannot discuss that with you. I can't believe that Cavendish would be so gauche as to involve you in this matter. He is a hotheaded fool, and instead of thinking about you and the consequences, he chose to challenge me. Does he know you are here now?" he demanded in frigid tones that turned her insides to jelly.

When Fiona shook her head mutely, he said, "May I remind you that your presence here was the reason he has called me out in the first place? You must leave at once. I am terribly sorry that our proposed duel has brought you grief, but I cannot help you."

"It is my actions that sparked this duel, and that's why I must stop it." Fiona rose to her feet as well. "Philip, please don't fight him. Ted was gravely injured in the war. He is ailing still and has been confined to his bed the past few days with a fever. Only the appearance of your seconds has prompted him to leave his bed prematurely. I will never forgive myself if anything were to happen to him because of my foolishness."

He did not respond but walked to the fireplace and stood there gazing into the flickering flames, his brow furrowed. Fiona looked at his unyielding back and continued to plead her case, hoping to thaw his icelike demeanor.

"Ted is very weak still. The last time the two of you dueled, he was laid up for months. Surely you will not put me through that agony again." She swallowed the lump in her throat and blinked back her tears as she faced him bravely. Her eyes begged him to acknowledge that he understood her intent, that he knew her concern was not only for her brother but for him as well. He stared back at her, not revealing any discernible emotion, and when he finally spoke, his voice was inflectionless and flat—almost bored.

"It was your brother who challenged. You were there. You witnessed it. I cannot in honor withdraw. I wish that I could if only to spare you further grief, but please accept my apologies. Maybe you could make your brother understand that I am not your lover and that what he witnessed was a moment of foolishness I sincerely regret. He might be persuaded to withdraw his challenge if he knew the truth." His words doused any flickering hopes of his affection for her. As they washed over her like ice-cold water, her heart sank. She couldn't stop the audible gasp as the love in her heart floundered. But even as she fought with her own emotions, she knew she couldn't give up. Too much lay in the balance. So, she gathered every vestige of courage, swallowed her pride, and renewed her appeal to him.

"I have tried to tell him that there is nothing between us, but he believes you were intent on seducing me and only his timely arrival stopped you. Your reputation does not help. Please, Philip, you can stop this. You are an honorable gentleman, surely you will not want to fight an ailing man who has suffered a recent injury. How can you be so cruel? Have you no compassion?" Her emotional outburst incited no change in Philip. His expression remained unmoved. If anything, he looked more cynical, if that were possible.

"Please, sir, I beseech you." Fiona ran and fell to her knees before him, tears streaming down her face. "This is all my fault, and if I had not run away from home, none of this would have happened. I cannot have the death of my brother on my conscience. You must help me!"

Philip reached down and raised her to her feet. "But why must you assume that he will die," he said softly. "I have no desire to kill him, and Ted is a fine fighting man who is excellent with both pistols and the sword. Do not despair, my lovely one, for it might be I who will die at your brother's hands."

Fiona registered the endearment he had offered but assumed that he was mocking her. His words, far from consoling her, caused her to sob even more. "You say that you do not intend to kill my brother," she cried. "Like you said, he is a fine duelist. What if you have no choice? I cannot bear it. Please, my lord, take pity on this wretched girl."

How it happened, she couldn't say, but one minute he was holding her away, and in the next she was clasped tightly against his chest, crying her heart out against his starched cravat. She clung to him as he held her close. The next few moments were both bliss and agony for her. Bliss to be in his arms, and agony because she thought he felt nothing for her.

Slowly, Fiona's sobbing ceased, and she pushed herself away to peep up at him. There was no sign of cynicism left in his face, only a deep sadness. Philip took out his handkerchief and gently wiped at her tears. "You say that you do not intend to kill my brother." She sniffed. "You know as well as I do that he is a fine duelist. What if you have no choice? I cannot bear it. Please have pity on me."

He remained silent as she stepped away from his arms to look up at him. His expression was unreadable, so she took her courage in her hands and continued. "If I cannot appeal to you as a gentleman not to fight my brother," she said resolutely, "I am willing by any other means to persuade you." And still with that look of determination on her face, she slowly unbuttoned the bodice of her gown.

"What exactly are you offering, my sweet?" he drawled silkily, drawing closer to her, but she stood her ground.

"You may have me in exchange for my brother's life." Her voice wobbled with uncertainty even as she spoke with defiance. She slipped her gown slowly from her shoulders.

His eyes never left her face. "What do you propose I do with you?" he prompted.

Fiona felt warmth flood her face. She did not know what she had expected him to do. Accept her offer and become the villain the ton painted him, or declare his love for her, shower her with kisses, and pledge to spare her brother? Whatever she had thought, reality was nothing like it. He made no move at all. He just stood there observing her with apparent amusement as she blushed from the top of her head down to her toes. Feeling gauche for the first time in her life, she was desperate to provoke a response from him. She batted her eyes at him with her best imitation of a come-hither smile, as she imagined a coquet would do.

His eyes seemed to bore into hers as he stood there looking like a panther stalking its prey. She stepped closer, but still he made no move to touch her.

"Make love to me," she whispered tremulously.

"Tempting as that sounds, I don't enjoy bedding reluctant maidens," he drawled, his smile widening.

"I am not reluctant. You could teach me? I will do whatever it takes to please you."

She knew she sounded desperate. She moved closer and leaned toward him until his lips were close to her. He bent down until his breath warmed her ears.

"Will you? Really, darling?" he whispered in dulcet tones.

Startled at the endearment, she looked up into his eyes but could not see past the darkness that masked them. He was not making this easy for her. She would have to show him that she meant what she said. Standing on tiptoe, she placed her arms around his neck and drew his face down to hers for a kiss.

The kiss took her breath away. She had expected to hate it and instead found herself wanting more. Wonder filled her as she acknowledged the feelings the kiss evoked in her. Butterflies fluttered in her stomach, and her entire being tingled with the awareness of his hard, male body so close to her own that her toes curl. Feeling breathless and lightheaded, she instinctively tightened her clasp around his neck to draw him even closer. She felt his lips yield to hers and felt the warmth of his body surround her. His masculine scent ignited her senses and made her want more. She clung to him as if she could not let go. But soon her common sense intervened, and her mind told her that he was not behaving in any way as a lover should. She had expected him to crush her to him, to cover her face with kisses, but he just stood there and allowed her to kiss him. So, she broke the kiss with reluctance and looked up into his face questioningly.

His lips curved in a mirthless smile that did not touch his eyes as he looked down at her. "What a remarkably interesting experience! I normally prefer my ladies with a bit of experience in bed, not green girls who are just out of the schoolroom. But there is some novelty in innocence, I guess, just not for me," he drawled.

Fiona blushed a fiery red as she realized he was mocking her. With a gasp of mortification, she spun away from him, setting her gown to rights. Humiliation ignited fury, and she lashed back at him. "You, sir, are not only a lecher but a murderer as well!" She raged. "I should not have expected any kindness from you, my lord, knowing your past and the fate of your poor wife. How deluded to expect you to have compassion? Have you not once already tried to put an end to Ted? Will you not be satisfied until he is dead? I should have known better than to come here to appeal to one such as you."

"You are right. You should not have come here. If your brother knew, he would call me out yet again, and our first duel is yet to happen. I cannot devote any more time to these affairs, I am a busy man," he said with a condescending smirk, pouring himself a drink from the amber whisky decanter.

With tears of rage and mortification welling up in her eyes, Fiona turned to leave, accepting defeat.

"Never despair, my pretty one," he called after her. "In a few years, once you are safely wed to some unsuspecting peer, I may be inclined to consider your delicious offer, if you are still of the same mind then."

Shaking with fury, Fiona swept from the room without a backward glance. Her emotions were in turmoil as she drove herself back to Red Oaks. The clouds cast an ominous shadow as she pondered the very dismal outcome of her visit. She had offered herself to him in all earnestness, believing that he desired her and that he was capable of some tenderness. The lecher had mocked her instead. The wretch! He had a heart of stone and the mind of a philanderer. It would serve him right if Ted drove his sword through him a dozen times. The tears that she had restrained until then burst forth and blinded her as she returned to Red Oaks at breakneck speed.

CHAPTER ELEVEN

Philip's mind churned as he kept rehashing Fiona's visit over and over, downing several glasses of brandy as he tried to calm his shot nerves.

His delight at seeing her had soon been replaced by dismay as he understood her purpose in visiting him. While her emotional plea had moved him as nothing before had, he had been helpless to agree to her request. He had felt about an inch tall, the veritable villain for distressing her so. If only he had not been weak, if only Ted had not found her in his arms. What a dilemma! How he longed to take her in his arms and kiss away her tears. What foolishness! Cursing his own weakness, he had steeled himself to remain unmoved. Desperate to hide his feelings, he had tried to act the cynical villain that he was rumored to be.

When she had tried to seduce him and offer herself in exchange for Ted's life, it had been a cruel knife twist to his heart. If she had kicked him in the gut, it would have hurt less. So, that was her true opinion of him. She regarded him as a rake and libertine with no honor. He had been frozen in shock as the full import of her words and actions sank in. She had obviously expected him to fall on her and ravish her, for she seemed uncertain what to do. If he weren't so angry, he would have found the whole situation absurd, even funny. However, it felt more like a contrived farce with him as an unwillingly cast villain. It had been torture to watch her play the role of a doxy for his benefit. Trying to piece together his shattered self-esteem, he had allowed his temper to become his shield. How dare she think him so low. If she thought him a rake, he certainly knew how to play one. He had unleashed his rage, seeking to hurt her as she had hurt him. He had forced himself to stay emotionless so she would not know how much she had hurt him, and then she had surprised him further by initiating a kiss.

That kiss had been mind-blowing. It had taken all of his self-control to keep his hands to his sides. All his resolve to be unmoved melted, as he had given himself without reserve to her kiss. How her lips had met and clung to his like sweet nectar. Her warm fragrance of summer flowers had encased him in a caress so gentle, and yet it had stirred feelings so ardent that he had been surprised. He thought that part of him was dead and buried with his late wife. He had been swept in a tide of longing to hold Fiona, to possess her, to make her his. His body had responded to her nearness, and blood had pounded in his veins, until he couldn't think or even breathe. His lips had involuntarily deepened the kiss with a hunger that he did not recognize.

Only his rigid self-control had prevented him from acting on his desire. It had been undiluted torture to restrain himself, but by reminding himself of their situation, and the reasons behind her actions, he had somehow managed to retain his self-control. Anger had returned as he recalled that her opinion of him was so poor that she had expected him to lay down his honor to bed her. His lips had stiffened then, and she must have sensed it, for she had stepped away from him, breaking their kiss.

He had wanted to hurt her then, for questioning his honor, for bruising his ego, for toying with his love. And he had. How her eyes had flashed with fiery anger and hurt. How she had renounced him and departed with her head held high even while tears had brightened her eyes to liquid, emerald lakes. He had felt such despair that he had wanted to throw himself at her feet and apologize for his words, but he knew that to do that meant exposing his feelings to her. And that path was not only doomed but also one of no return. So, he had let her leave thinking him the darkest libertine. She was not to know that the man she left behind was a broken one. Torn between his feelings for her and the need to defend his honor, her departure had left him shrouded in despair. His world had clouded with gloom, as he had stood there, shoulders slumped, for an eternity, staring sightlessly at nothing. When he eventually returned to his desk, he could do no more than stare blindly at the papers in front of him. Then he had reached for his decanter and drowned his pain.

At dawn the next morning, after a sleepless night spent in an armchair staring into the dying embers of the fire in his study, he dressed himself and drove in his carriage to the appointed spot for the duel. He felt numb and weary even as he questioned Cavendish's logic in choosing a spot close to Red Oaks but quite far from Crossfields. As the carriage drew near, he saw that two other vehicles were already waiting. He recognized one as the carriage of his friend Cameron and breathed a sigh of relief that his seconds had come in time. The second carriage must have been Cavendish's or one of his seconds.

As he alighted, the occupants of the other two carriages did likewise. He saw Cameron and Hector, his seconds, and Cavendish with Captain Colin Sanders and Major Timothy Firth. The surgeon was not there yet.

Hector and Timothy went off to check the ground, leaving the two adversaries to inspect the swords.

"You had the choice of weapons, Phil. With your reputation as a crack shot, I am surprised you chose swords," Cam remarked. "You know that Cavendish is damn good with swords."

"I had my reasons," Philip said softly. He inspected his colichemarde and pronounced it satisfactory. He looked up to see that Ted Cavendish had paused in his own inspection, regarding him with a quizzical expression.

Philip looked away and complained with impatience at the delay caused by the doctor. At that moment, the doctor's carriage rattled in, and the duelists proceeded to the selected piece of turf to commence the dual.

Sheffield and Cavendish both removed their coats and turned up their cuffs, and facing each other, they saluted with their swords in customary fashion.

"First blood, gentlemen?" Colin asked. Philip glanced at Ted, who nodded assent.

Cavendish shouted, "En garde," and the duel began.

Ted attacked immediately with a lunge, which Philip effectively parried, and that set the tone of the battle. Ted mounted a strong offensive while Philip stayed on defense. It was obvious to all who watched that the adversaries were very evenly matched.

"Surely they can't keep up that pace," Timothy remarked anxiously.

"Ted is still a trifle pulled, and his strength will give out soon if he keeps that up."

Cavendish fought with a blazing intensity while Philip responded with a lazy and almost careless ease. Neither gave an inch, but several times it seemed that Cavendish almost had Philip, who deflected his opponent's blade in the nick of time. The duel raged on, becoming more heated and furious with every passing minute. Cavendish, who was not fully recovered from his battle wound and weakened further by the infection, started to tire soon. Sweat broke out on his forehead with the exertion, and knowing he wouldn't last long, he started taking more risks and became decidedly rash in his attack. Now the tide turned, and it was apparent to all the onlookers that the advantage was with Philip, but strangely he did not seem to avail it.

"Watch out, Ted," Colin shouted to Cavendish as Philip's sword almost hit home but was deflected at the last minute.

"The deuce! What is Phil playing at? He could have easily had him that time too," Cameron exclaimed after a very intense few minutes of parries and thrusts.

Philip realized that Ted was running out of steam, but his temper appeared to have only heated. He was taking foolish risks that Philip could have used to his advantage and ended the duel several times, but something held him back. He knew that Ted would not desist until he had drawn blood and also knew that he was playing with fire, but his mood was very black. In his mind, he kept seeing the vision of raging yet tear-filled, green eyes that had flashed at him in anger and aversion, and he became increasingly more reckless with each onslaught. He did not care about the outcome anymore, he just fought because he found the duel exhilarating and wanted to prolong the rush. He wanted the challenge and exertion of the fight to erase the hurt Fiona had caused with her parting words. The exhilaration of dueling was a salve for his injured pride, and he fought with a nonchalance that was foreboding.

Miscalculating that Ted was at the end of his tether, he became more cavalier in his defense. Ted's next thrust was unexpected and well-timed: just when Philip lowered his guard. It was true and drove home. His sword sliced through Philip's shirt and through his body. With a shout, the seconds ran up, but Ted had already wrenched his sword out and stepped back. Philip realized dazedly that he was hit. His vision blurred, and his sword fell from his nerveless fingers as the deadly splotch of blood spread on his chest, turning his shirt crimson. Blackness engulfed his vision, erasing the green eyes that had haunted him. His last thought as he sank to the ground was the regret that he would not see those eyes ever again.

———◇———

Ted watched in a detached way as the surgeon rushed up and tended to his adversary. The remainder of the evening took on a surreal appearance. Philip collapsed, and Cameron ran up to support him before his head touched the ground. The duel had taken far longer than expected, and the fatigue that adrenaline had kept at bay now made its presence known. Early into the duel, he had realized that his injury was a severe impediment, and that he was very much outmatched. He had expected to lose, and lose quickly, but then it had dawned on him that his opponent was toying with him and trying to wear him down, and that had fueled his smoldering anger. He had resolved to teach Sheffield a lesson, and summoning every ounce of strength remaining, he had attacked fiercely, seeking only to injure his opponent. Now seeing Sheffield prone on the ground with a bloodied chest, his anger abated as the realization that he had won sank in. He marveled that despite the fierce fight his opponent had put up, he hadn't suffered so much as a scratch. He expected to feel elation at his victory, but instead he felt cheated.

Have I killed Philip? he wondered. The thought surprisingly filled him with such regret that he went closer to where the doctor was tending to his fallen adversary.

The surgeon, Dr. Carver, deftly applied pressure and bound up Philip's wound with expertise. Philip remained unconscious through it all. The surgeon looked grim when he turned to the men, who were anxiously awaiting his verdict.

"He is not dead," he declared, and the others breathed a collective sigh of relief. "His wound is very deep, but I think it has missed his vital organs. He has lost a lot of blood already, and I am unable to staunch the flow completely. He needs to be stitched up at once, and I have neither the tools nor the facilities to do that here. We must take him somewhere quickly where I may tend to him, or I cannot vouch for his survival."

"Let's go to my house," Lord Hector Bainbridge offered immediately. "It's fairly close, and my staff can help take care of him."

"No! Mine is closer." Everyone turned in surprise to look at Ted, who had spoken. "My house, Red Oaks, is closer, and my housekeeper is a skilled nurse."

"Hold up, mate," Cameron protested. "It isn't the done thing, you know. Can't very well take a man you just dueled into your home to mend. That flouts all protocol."

"Protocol be dammed," Ted swore succinctly. "You heard the sawbones. Sheffield dies if his wound is not tended to right away. I am loath to be obliged to leave my beloved home and country, should this make-bait bleed to death, which he is bound to do just to spite me, while you are trying to get him to your dammed estate in godforsaken country. How about if you all stop standing about jawing and instead give me a hand to put him into his carriage?" He spoke with the voice that the men under his command in the military knew brooked no argument.

Cameron looked at Hector, who appeared just as surprised at this turn of events. Hector gave a quick nod of assent. Without further ado, he and Cameron, with Colin and Timothy's aid, supported Philip and carried him to his carriage. Cavendish and Timothy boarded Cavendish's carriage and drove out in haste, followed by Sheffield's carriage containing the fallen man, the doctor, and Hector. Cameron followed in his own carriage, and the doctor's vehicle driven by Colin completed the procession that rapidly made its way to Red Oaks.

CHAPTER TWELVE

The sun had come up when the procession of carriages entered the Red Oaks estate. Fiona, who had been unable to sleep, was already at the breakfast table nursing a cup of coffee when she heard the sound of the carriages pulling up. She ran quickly to the entry hall in time to see a prone figure being carried in, supported by Hector and Colin. She couldn't see his face but saw that his shirt was stained crimson. Her immediate thought was that her brother was hurt, and she gave a cry of anguish. Then she saw Ted walking behind them, looking drawn and weary but unhurt. She knew then that he was safe and offered a prayer of thanks, but at the same time she realized that the injured man must be Philip. She felt a sharp pang of anguish that he should be seriously injured.

Not stopping to examine why she should feel such grief at that lecher being hurt, she ran up to the men just as Ted instructed the assembled servants to prepare a guest room and help carry the wounded man there. He asked his butler, Sudbury, to ensure that water be heated and linen be prepared for bandages and to alert the housekeeper, Mrs. Kibble, that her assistance was required by the doctor.

"Oh, Ted! Thank God you are safe! Are you hurt? What happened? Is he dead?" Fiona exclaimed, clutching Ted's hand.

"He's still alive but badly hurt. The surgeon said he wouldn't survive unless he was tended to immediately, so I brought him here." Ted answered her last question first. He looked into her worried face and interpreting the anguish in her face and the tears pooling in her eyes, said kindly, "Never fret, love. I am unhurt, merely fatigued."

His words did little to reassure Fiona, who suddenly felt faint as the events of the last few days finally caught up with her. She would have fallen if Cavendish had not caught her and guided her to a chair. He pushed her head down into her knees and knelt next to her.

In a moment, the dizziness passed, and Fiona sat up and looked tearfully at her brother's concerned face. "Oh! How terrible if Sheffield should die. You will have to flee the country, and I will be left all alone again. I could not bear to live without you." She sobbed. Or *him,* prompted a little thought in her head that she heard but chose to ignore.

Ted pulled her into his arms and let her sob on his shoulder. "There is no chance of that, little one. The lecherous cad will survive, and I won't be fleeing to France any time soon," he said comfortingly. Fiona offered up a silent prayer that he should speak truly.

The surgeon spent a long time in Philip's room with the door closed. Mrs. Kibble helped him in cleaning and stitching up the wound. When finally he came downstairs, he found several people awaiting him anxiously. He recognized all the men from the duel, but his heart went out to the girl who looked so distressed. He was touched by the concern and grief in her eyes. Being a romantic soul, he concluded that the wounded man was her lover. He unwittingly addressed her as he gave his diagnosis.

Philip had not regained consciousness through his ministrations but was out of danger for the present. The sword had slipped on his ribs and toward the middle of his torso but had thankfully missed all the vital organs, but he had lost a lot of blood and needed to rest. The doctor recommended that the wounded man be under constant care, as he still could take a turn for the worse. He said that he would send a nurse to care for him. He gave detailed instructions about the care of the patient and asked that he be summoned immediately at any sign of fever, as that could signal infection. Under no circumstance was Philip to be moved for at least a week, he cautioned, or the consequences would be dire. He had administered laudanum to the wounded man, as much rest was needed. The patient would be asleep for long periods of time, he indicated.

The young men all looked at Ted, who passed a tired hand through his already-rumpled hair and promised to follow all the doctor's directions to the letter. The doctor left after declining an offer of breakfast. Hector and Cameron also took their leave after promising to stop and check on the patient later. Colin and Tim breakfasted with Ted and his sister and left shortly after.

As soon as the guests departed, Fiona followed her brother upstairs. Ted hesitated outside Philip's door and then went in, and Fiona followed. They found Mrs. Kibble sitting next to the bed, and she left the room when they entered. Philip looked like he was in a deep sleep. His face was very pale but peaceful. His normally severe hairstyle was disheveled, and his dark hair fell over his brow in unruly waves that gave him a surprisingly youthful appearance. He was draped in blankets up to his waist, but his chest was exposed. Fiona could see the thick bandages that bound his torso. She also noticed an old scar on his shoulder, which she recognized as a bullet wound. She looked at Ted, who stood staring at the wounded man broodingly. She wondered what had made him bring Philip to Red Oaks to recover.

As if hearing her thoughts, Ted spoke. "The fool!" he muttered. "He could have had me at least a half a dozen times but held back. I only got him finally because he had lowered his guard. It's almost like he wanted me to win. When he wakes up, he'll have to answer to me for that."

With that he turned and left the room, forgetting his sister. Fiona pulled the sheets gently to cover Philip's chest and smoothed them over him. Then she followed her brother out of the room, leaving Mrs. Kibble to resume her vigil until the nurse arrived. The rest of the day she was somber as she pondered the incomprehensible ways of males and wondered how it was that a man could think nothing of bringing his wounded enemy home and yet contemplate fighting the same enemy for sparing his life. And why had Philip allowed himself to lose the duel? By all accounts Philip was the more skilled duelist and also in better form than Ted, who was hampered by his injury. Could it be because of her plea to him? Had he put his own life at risk to spare her brother? Why? Surely not for her sake? He had made it clear that he harbored no tender sentiment for her and did not even desire her. Men! What exasperating creatures they were!

CHAPTER THIRTEEN

The doctor sent a competent nurse to care for the patient. Samuels had also arrived promptly as soon as heard about his master's injury. He and Mrs. Kibble took turns to relieve the nurse and sit by the patient. Philip did not regain consciousness that day. Toward evening, the much-dreaded fever set in, and the doctor was summoned again. The doctor found him burning and delirious. He would not give them any hope and said that only time would tell, but he looked very grim.

Neither Fiona nor Ted got any rest that night. Ted, fatigued as he was, couldn't rest. His mind kept turning over the duel, and he remained brooding aimlessly in his room, feeling useless until he could take it no longer. He decided to go check on the patient. He found the nurse looking tired and Philip tossing about restless. Ted ordered her to go to the kitchen to have some tea and take a break from her duties while he stayed with Philip for a while. The nurse gratefully left the room after promising to return soon.

He settled himself in a chair by the fire, and his thoughts wandered to the duel and then to the man lying unconscious. He and Philip Merton had met at Eton and had remained friends even at Cambridge. They had been close in their youth, falling into scrapes. They had done all the usual things that young men were wont to do when they had no responsibilities. They had encountered Lady Elizabeth Sheridan at a ball given by Lady Sefton, and both young men had fallen in love at once. Lady Elizabeth was declared a diamond of the first water, upon making her debut to the London ton. With the face of an angel and the figure of a Greek goddess, she captivated one and all with her carriage and charm. Her smile was infectious and soon made her popular with the younger set.

Ted and Phil had vied with each other in showering her with their attentions. They haunted her home every morning, took her for drives, and danced with her at all the assemblies. They even ventured into Almack's just so they could be in her company. After a whirlwind courtship, Elizabeth had accepted Philip's offer. The friendship between Ted and Philip had become strained after the wedding.

Phil's father had suffered a heart ailment, and Philip had repaired to Crossfields with his bride to sort out his affairs. Dejected that his love had been rejected, Ted's sorrow had been even more intensified with the unfortunate loss of his parents. Their carriage had overturned on the way to Red Oaks. Cousin Sadie had arrived in his hour of need to take charge of the household. Within a few months, Fiona had been dismissed to a finishing school. Finding time hanging on his hands, Ted had signed up to serve in the military.

Even away in the peninsula, the rumors had reached him that his friend's marriage was not a happy one. On one of his leaves, he had found Elizabeth in residence at the Sheffield home in Berkley, while Philip remained at Crossfields. Paying a call to the lady Sheffield, he had spied bruises on her fair arms that gave credence to the ugly rumors that Philip had taken to beating his beautiful wife. He had chosen to believe the stories that Philip had been abusive to that gentle creature. Very soon thereafter, Lady Elizabeth had met with an untimely death. There had been an investigation, and news had reached him again that she had been with child and had met her end at her jealous husband's hands. Philip was rumored to have barely escaped with his life, having sustained a gunshot wound on his shoulder. The insinuation was that Elizabeth had tried to defend herself in her last moments and had tragically failed. Though an inquest was conducted, Philip's name had been cleared.

Enraged that his gentle love had been thus treated, Ted had called Philip out. Their duel had been fierce and well-matched. Philip had won, and Ted had been forced to take to his bed with his injury. His recovery had been slow.

With his reputation in shreds, the honorable Philip Merton had retreated to Crossfields. The ton had mourned the loss of their darling

Lady Elizabeth by painting him with a tarred brush. There was no debauchery that had not been attributed to Phil's name, no vile offense that he had not been accused of. The haut ton had unanimously closed their doors to him.

It was funny how all that had changed once he had succeeded to his father's title. The ton had immediately forgiven him his sins in light of his new fortune. Many caps were set at him, but as Philip seldom ventured into London and almost never accepted invitations to social engagements, he had remained elusive. The thwarted matrons had in spite set about rumors of his many mistresses. Most gentlemen, Ted included, had never paid heed to these. Philip had maintained his reputation as a sportsman of repute. He was considered a top sawyer by his peers, and when he occasionally was glimpsed about London, his attire and style were much remarked and emulated. Ted, though aware that Philip was well received and that his close friends had stayed true to him through all the rumor and gossip, had continued to think the worst of him. Recalling now the concern evidenced by both Cameron and Hector at the duel and remembering the man he had once called his friend, Ted began to question the validity of all the stories regarding Philip's ill-fated marriage.

He was roused from his thoughts by Philip crying out in his insentient state. Rising, he approached the bed to find the incumbent man delirious and incoherent. He appeared to be lost in the throes of a bad dream. The words were slurred, mumbled, and barely comprehensible, but one name caught his attention: Elizabeth. Over and over, Philip seemed to be calling out to her, pleading almost. Philip's voice rose as he kept calling out to his dead wife; his body tossed, flinging off the covers and almost falling off the bed. Suddenly, after an anguished "No," his body went still. Ted feared that the end had come and that Philip had drawn his last breath. Bending to check for a pulse, he found that Philip still lived but had sunk into a deep slumber. Ted touched his forehead and discovered it bathed in sweat but cool. The nurse returned then and said she would wipe Philip's face with a cool cloth. As Ted turned to leave the room, Philip called out again. He froze in his tracks as Philip softly but distinctly said one word: "Fiona."

Ted drew his breath in sharply at the sound of his sister's name. He suspected that Fiona had feelings for Philip that she may not herself be yet aware of. And from what he had just witnessed, it looked like Philip held his sister in his affections as well. A problem he had not anticipated. Philip, with his scandalous past, could not be allowed to marry Fiona and drag her down the path of disgrace. Fiona needed to marry right away, or she would forfeit her inheritance and her independence along with it. Knowing his sister, she would only marry for love, and if her affections were inclined toward Philip, then there was only heartache in store for her.

Disturbed, Ted returned to his room and bed. He couldn't put what he had just heard and witnessed out of his mind. He had believed that Philip had taken his rage out on Elizabeth, who in fear had run and fallen down the stairs and died. But what he had just witnessed revealed a quite different Philip from the one the gossips had painted. He had seen a man very much in love with his wife and who had been devastated by her death. So what was the truth? Had his jealousy of Philip for marrying Elizabeth clouded his judgment? Had he wrongfully believed that Philip was responsible for Elizabeth's death? Ted decided that he would get to the bottom of this puzzle as well. Philip owed him more than one explanation. That farce of a duel, now this, and, last but not least, his intentions toward his sister. It was in a very grim mood that Ted retired to bed, but sleep continued to elude him.

While Ted was immersed in his ponderings, his sister was likewise preoccupied in her bed. Her conscience was busy in heaping guilt and self-recrimination on her head. She had convinced herself without a doubt that Philip had deliberately refrained from harming her brother because of her. And, in the bargain, he now lay at death's door. The doctor had looked very solemn when he had left late that night, and the fever had shown no sign of abating.

She had thought that she was doing the right thing in asking Philip to spare her brother, but now it could end up costing him his own life. If Philip should die, then she was as culpable as her brother, for though his had been the hand that held the sword, it was she who had sent him to his death. The thought of his death made her heart sink to the very pit of her belly, and a sense of desolation so dark clouded her mind that she couldn't breathe. Tears crept unbidden into her eyes and spilled down her pale cheeks. He had been kind to her and treated her gently; he did not deserve such a fate. And her brother thought him a villain who had attempted to seduce her against her will. She had to convince Ted of the truth. Why had she been such a hoyden and created a situation that had endangered not only her reputation but also the lives of two fine men who she cared about?

She caught herself as that thought registered. Yes! She did care about them both; one as a beloved brother and the other as . . . ? She had no immediate answer to that. But the rapid beat of her heart made her remember their last encounter, where she had offered herself to Philip, and the kiss she had initiated. Her cheeks flamed at the memory. She should feel anger or humiliation that he had refused her, but instead she felt a quiver of something else. Desire. An emotion that made her both excited and scared in a way that she had never experienced before. That episode would have to remain her secret, or it would only lead to more bad blood between the two men. Meanwhile the object of her affections was within her reach. She could see him every day if she so wished. And while he recovered, they would have a chance to get to know each other, a fate-given opportunity to spend time with each other. Perhaps this would allow Ted to see Philip for the gentleman he was to her. Her mind was made up. *Oh God, please let him recover!* she prayed silently as she tossed and turned in her bed.

CHAPTER FOURTEEN

Philip finally gained consciousness early the morning of the third day after the duel. When he woke, he had no idea where he was. The last thing he could remember was that stupid duel. Wait—Ted had run him through at the duel. Was he dead? No! This place did not look anything like heaven, or hell either, for that matter. He tried to raise himself but felt a sharp pain in his chest and sank back with a groan. No, he definitely was not dead, so he must be at one of his friend's places, though he could not recall how he got there. Weak, he closed his eyes again and thus missed seeing Mrs. Kibble, who had wakened by his cry and came to check on him and then went to fetch Ted.

Thus, it was that the next time Philip woke he found Cavendish standing next to his bed. He tried to sit up in outrage but fell back again as the pain overcame him.

"Stay still, you mad man! You have lost a lot of blood and are likely as weak as a kitten," Cavendish said, holding him down by his arms.

"What kind of villainy is this? You are not content with winning the duel, you have brought me here to torture me? Let me up." Philip gasped weakly.

"If I did torture you, it is no more than you deserve. It was not my desire to harbor you in my house either. The doctor said that if we did not act quickly you would die, and I did not want your death on my hands. I have no inclination to leave the country because of your stupidity."

"Did you bring me here to insult and torture me? Little do you care if I die. You were certainly bloodthirsty enough the other day when you found your sister in my arms." Philip again struggled to sit up and failed abysmally.

"That was before you so foolishly contrived to die by my sword rather than dueling as you should have," Edward retaliated, still holding him down by force.

"What fustian you speak!" Flushing, Philip struggled some more.

"Now stay still, damn you. I know that you let me win."

As his words registered, Philip stilled for a moment and then started struggling with renewed force.

"I don't know what drivel your sister has been feeding you, but I most certainly never fight to lose," he said.

"Leave my sister out of this." Edward's voice took a dangerous note.

"Hold your horses, man. God forbid, I don't need another duel." Suddenly exhausted, Philip gave up the struggle and lay still. "I can't stay here. It's not the done thing, surely even you must see that I ought to leave right away."

"I can't let you leave in the condition you are in. Dr. Carver says you are not to be moved on any account. Anyway, you have been here for three days. Another day or two will make no difference."

"Three days! You lie, the duel was only yesterday," Philip retorted.

"Touch your face if you don't believe me."

Philip, doing just that, exclaimed in surprise at the length of the coarse stubble his fingers encountered on his face. He looked at Edward, bewildered.

"Yes." Ted answered the unspoken question in his eyes, his voice low and subdued in contrast to the rancor in his words. "It was touch and go there for a while. You nearly turned up your toes with your stupid heroics and almost had me running for the border for having killed you."

He passed a hand over his eyes in a gesture that bespoke of weariness. "But you must rest now. We can discuss this later. I'll have Mrs. Kibble bring you some broth." Turning, he left the room.

Philip lay in bed wondering whether a very stubborn and intrepid girl had come clean about her part in the duel and just how much Ted actually knew about that encounter. Not everything, he hoped; he could not deal with another duel, for it would kill him.

He was not left alone for long. True to his word, Ted had Mrs.

Kibble bring Philip some broth, which he insisted on feeding himself and ended up spilling half on his sheets. Samuels was obliged to fetch fresh sheets, then shaved him at his insistence. After which he was paid a visit by the good doctor, who insisted on removing the bandages to inspect his wound, which proved to be a very unpleasant and painful experience. The doctor pronounced the wound healing nicely but that any movement would reopen it and bring the risk of infection back. Philip was to be confined to bed for another week. This diagnosis made Philip swear so profusely that Mrs. Kibble, who had assisted the doctor, hurriedly left the room with her hands over her ears. He then attempted to prove the doctor wrong by trying to get out of bed, only to fall back weakly in a sweat, unable to withstand the excruciating pain. The doctor grunted in disgust at his patient and followed Mrs. Kibble. Thoroughly spent, Philip closed his eyes, but visions of sparkling, green eyes kept flitting into his mind after he fell asleep.

When next he woke, it was evening. A fire had been lit in his room, and sitting by the fire was an angel in white. His first thought was that he had finally died, and she had been sent to guide him to heaven. He blinked as his eyes tried to focus on the heavenly apparition. Then the dancing flames of the fire caught the red highlights in her hair, and Philip knew that all angelic resemblance ended with the color of the gown she wore as he recognized Fiona. He belatedly clutched the blanket to his chin, trying to cover up his naked chest. His movement attracted Fiona's attention.

"There is no need to be bashful, my lord," she said as she approached the bed. "I know what a man's chest looks like having grown up with a brother. In any case, it's a bit late, as I have been sitting here for a while, as you were sleeping."

Flushed, Philip glared at her in horror and mortification. "Do you possess even an ounce of propriety, Miss Cavendish? Even you must know that an unmarried lady must never visit a gentleman's bedchamber, let alone admit to gazing at his uncovered chest while he is asleep. What is your brother thinking of to permit such behavior?"

His illness had made him drop his guard, and his mask of cynicism had slipped, leaving him exposed and vulnerable, and Fiona was determined to take full advantage of it. She drew closer and leaned over him. "Don't worry, no one knows I am here, so your bachelorhood is safe, and you won't have to offer for me," she said.

Philip shrank back, appalled. "God forbid! Miss Cavendish, you must leave at once. I beg you."

Coming closer still, she laid a cool hand on his forehead and smoothed the hair from his brow. "Not until I have thanked you for sparing my brother, my lord," she said, and before he could respond, she dropped a quick kiss on his forehead and stepped away.

Philip froze for a second, and then seeing the smile of mischief in her eyes, he swiftly recovered. Summoning his most bored demeanor, he said, "I have no idea of what you speak. I was careless, and Edward has always been the better swordsman, so it was inevitable that he should win. Now, if you do not mind, I would appreciate it if you left before you provoke another duel."

Fiona only laughed at him and straightened his blanket. "My poor man, you don't like being helpless, do you?"

"I am not helpless and am quite capable of delivering the spanking you deserve if your brother doesn't do it," Philip said with gritted teeth and a scowl like a thunder cloud, but she just laughed some more and traipsed to the door. Hand on handle, she turned and winked at him before she finally left. As the door closed with a faint click, he heard her giggle.

Philip relaxed and allowed himself to grin at her outrageous behavior. She was utterly unique, and the man who spent his life with her would never be bored. The next minute, he sobered, remembering that it would not be he who would spend his life with her but some other lucky man who was not burdened by a shadowed past.

The next two days were very trying for Philip, and for Ted's household as well. His wound was healing well, but the blood loss made him weak. The doctor recommended that he not navigate the stairs until he was stronger. And since he refused to be carried down the stairs, he was forced to remain at Red Oaks.

He was a poor patient and constantly complained and called the good doctor a quack. He sorely tried the patience of Mrs. Kibble and Samuels but was always truly kind to the maids who brought him food. To make things worse, Fiona was intent on creeping to his room despite his efforts to warn her off, though he treated her as he would a recalcitrant child, a fact that did not escape Edward's notice.

When the doctor finally pronounced him able to travel, a relieved Philip sent word to his host requesting a visit. Edward walked into Philip's room to find him sitting in an armchair and staring pensively at the fire. He did not hear Ted's knock, and it wasn't until Ted coughed right next to him that he realized he had a visitor.

Ted pulled up a chair and joined Philip across the fire. "I am glad to see that you are recovered," he said.

Philip's eyes held his usual bored expression. "Are you really? I had thought you wanted to see me dead. Anyway, it's past time that I should be gone from here. If you can send for my coach, I can cease to be a burden on you and your household," he said.

"It's not my household that concerns me," Edward responded, looking him in the eye. "'Tis my sister. I have seen the way she looks at you, and I am concerned."

"Your sister, Cavendish, is a darn pest," said Philip with the demeanor of a much-tried man. "I have asked her a thousand times to stay away, but she insists on inflicting her company on me. You really must keep her more in hand."

"Fiona sometimes can be as naïve as a child. She really does not know the ways of society or men. She has been left alone for far too long with her books and has some romantic notions in her head that may have gotten fanned to a flame by our duel. It is my fault entirely, but I don't want any hint of scandal to touch her life."

Philip felt his temper rise and spoke out without thinking. "You wrong your sister by describing her as such. She is strong and independent and knows her mind and speaks it. She is both brave and intelligent and capable of making her own decisions. In the short time of our acquaintance, I have learned that she has views on many subjects that are superior to many of the dandies you see in Mayfair."

Ted quirked an eyebrow upward at this unexpected defense of his sister. His fixed gaze made Philip color and fall silent.

"Sheffield, if you have any interest in my sister, then I must know the truth. I cannot allow that she be associated with a . . . a man of some notoriety, unless of course rumors lie and there is more to the situation than is known. Do you have some information that can provide some clarity to the . . . erm, situation?" Ted turned his hawklike stare onto his captive patient.

Philip met his stare steadily but remained silent for a long moment. His heart leapt with hope even as his mind pondered Ted's words. He was aware that Cavendish was offering him an olive branch. How he wished he could accept it. If only it were that simple! Cavendish's words spelled out his hidden doubts, and that made the situation impossible. Philip may not care about what others thought of him, but the fact that one of his oldest friends still believed him a villain rankled. He knew he was being unfair and that Ted was only doing what any brother would do in demanding an explanation. However, it was not an explanation that his code of honor permitted Philip to divulge. His code was the one thing that had helped him endure the scandal that had followed his wife's death and the life of a pariah that had become his in the aftermath. He had found consolation in the thought that he had and was doing the right thing. How could he now break his own code as a gentleman, just so he could marry again? It was selfish, and he could not bring himself to do it. Therefore, he shook his head regretfully.

"There's nothing to tell," he said. "Rumor speaks truly in my case, and I am indeed the lecher I am painted to be. You are wise to keep your sister away from me, as I have nothing to offer her except a ruined reputation."

Ted stared at him for several moments with a furrowed brow, as if the words baffled him. Then he nodded acknowledgment and left the room without a word.

CHAPTER FIFTEEN

Fiona frowned as she walked about the garden listlessly. The garden of beautiful shrubs was filled with the trilling of mating birds, but its beauty was lost on her. Her shoulders slumped, and her brow furrowed, and she chewed on her lips as she walked about in circles. Ted's return had meant she could officially enter London society. She had attended many parties and balls and had acquired a fan following. Flowers arrived every day from all her attentive admirers. Her entourage of beaus was a balm to her vanity.

But while she reveled in all the adulation, when left alone she found herself despondent. She was flattered by the pretty posies, but she didn't feel any delight at the thought that she was popular. Instead, while she outwardly welcomed the attention, her heart remained aloof. While out in society, she behaved just as was expected of her. She attended parties and went for rides with friends. She flirted with all her many beaus. But each night she sighed knowing her heart was not into it. It was not that she was choosy or that she demanded a lot from her suitors. It was that she did not feel anything toward the most handsome or titled young men who flocked to her side.

Instead, her mind wandered to a dark, cynical face, and she found herself wondering what he was doing. However much she tried to distract herself by laughing and flirting with her beaus, her thoughts kept returning to the one gentleman who had not sent any word at all. None!

She sighed deeply as she continued on her perambulations. She was in poor spirits and did not know why. The wretched rake had left Red

Oaks two weeks ago without so much as a farewell. Surely that was not why she felt so glum. In fact, she was genuinely happy to see him go! He was always criticizing her and treating her like a child. She did not miss him . . . or did she?

Why had Philip not sent word? Despite his cold behavior before the duel where she had disastrously attempted to kiss him, she suspected that he had warm feelings for her. He must have refused her offer and been unpleasant about it just to deter her. However, during his recovery when he had been unconscious, she had heard him mumble her name more than once. A man only called out to a woman he had feelings for at his most vulnerable, did he not? Given, he had also called out his first wife's name with equal if not more frequency. But that meant nothing, only that he had loved her, which only confirmed her theory that the rumors about his first marriage were not entirely true. She had not imagined his face lighting up whenever he saw her, even though he had protested her presence at his bedside. Why, then, had he left without a word? Had Ted warned him off? If that was the case, what was she to do?

"A penny for them?" Fiona looked up to see Ted standing next to her, looking at her with a smile. She had not heard him approach.

Fiona smiled back, glad to see him looking well. "I was just woolgathering," she said. They continued walking together.

"Are you excited about attending the Langton ball next week?" Ted inquired.

"Yes, I am, and you are a dear for agreeing to take me. I know how you hate these affairs."

"Do you mind that Cousin Sadie and Cousin Harry will be there, chickee?"

"Not if it makes you happy, dear," she said, attempting to smile without much success.

"Fiona, you do know that I only want your happiness. I would never expect you to marry Harry Albrighton. He is nothing but a spoiled dandy and pockets to let, besides. But they are still family, and he is my heir, and we must keep up appearances. You only need to be civil. Anyway, you will be too busy dancing the evening away to worry about poor old Harry. And I'll keep Cousin Sadie out of your hair."

"That sounds wonderful, dearest." Fiona leaned and kissed her brother. And Ted hugged her affectionately.

Then he stopped and turned her to face him. "There's something else I must tell you," he said. She looked at him questioningly, surprised by the sudden seriousness of his voice.

"Your birthday is approaching fast, and if you are not married soon, your inheritance will be forfeited and passed on to Cousin Margaret, Uncle Henry's daughter, who, as you know, is wed and has a brood of rug rats already. So, you have a decision to make, dearest. Is there anyone among your many worthy suitors who you can consider wedding?"

Fiona's face reflected her dismay. "Ted, you know I will not wed except for love . . ." Her voice trailed off.

"I know that, dear girl, but that would mean you will relinquish your inheritance and your independence. I am more than happy to make you an allowance for life from Papa's estate if that is what you wish, but if I should die, it will not surprise me if my heir turns mean-spirited and cuts you off. I cannot be at ease knowing your future to be uncertain. I know you had hoped to travel and see the world and do good work with your inheritance, and I do not like to see your dreams dying prematurely. Is there not someone you can consider, sweetheart?"

His words caused a dark, cynical face to flit into her mind, prompting her cheeks to bloom a rosy pink. She dropped her gaze, shaking her head.

"Very well then, not to worry, chick. I will try to live to a ripe old age and take care of you," Ted said, chucking her chin affectionately.

"You mean I will be the one taking care of you, my dearest brother?" Fiona responded, recovering her composure with a laugh.

Ted laughed with her at that, and giving her an affectionate hug, turned to leave, saying, "By the by, Philip Merton is invited to the ball as well. Will his presence there distress you?"

"Distress? No, why should I be distressed by him? I will be most surprised if he accepts. After all, he is seldom seen in society." Fiona spoke lightly, but inside her butterflies of hope fluttered in her belly, and at the same time a coil of dread unfurled at the thought that he may not want to see her. It was thus with both eagerness and reluctance that she received the news of her impending encounter with the man who haunted her dreams. She noticed that Ted was watching her closely, so she smiled and shrugged to keep him from divining her feelings.

THE HOYDEN AND THE RAKE

"Langton is his bosom beau, so he cannot refuse." Ted still looked at her with concern as he continued. "Chickee, I am off to town today, would you like to go?"

"You go on, dear. I have to attend to the seamstress about the alterations to my gown. Also, my school friend, Amy Arlington, is arriving tomorrow. So, I must stay and prepare for her visit and welcome her," she said. "You remember Amy, do you not, Ted?"

Ted nodded, but she could tell that he did not remember her friend very well. However, the look of worry that she had noticed in his eyes was replaced with relief. She watched him return to the house before returning to the turmoil within. She had to look her best at the ball, she decided, then perhaps Philip would know his heart and approach her, perhaps even offer for her. If that were to happen . . . her heart beat so loudly like a big bass drum at the very thought, she feared that Ted would hear. A smile like a ray of sunshine breaking through the clouds lit up her face, and the world around her glowed like a rainbow again.

CHAPTER SIXTEEN

Miss Amy Arlington arrived the next day. Fiona greeted her friend with apparent delight and enfolded her in a warm embrace that spoke volumes about their relationship.

Amy was the only girl in a family of men. Her father had made his fortune with the East India Company in India, and her mother had been the daughter of an Indian maharaja, a princess in her own right. Amy's mother had died in India during childbirth, and Amy had been sent to live with relatives in Bath by her father. She had attended the same boarding school as Fiona. The two girls had been drawn to each other and had become remarkably close. They regarded each other more as family than as friends and had remained in touch even after they had left the finishing school more than a year ago. It had been a while since they had seen each other, as Amy had returned to Bath to take care of an ailing aunt right after seminary, and Fiona had gone to London to stay with her cousin Sadie.

Amy was as different from Fiona as apples from pears. She had wide, brown eyes and smooth, brown hair—which was never out of place— and a shy smile. She presented a well-groomed and serene demeanor. Amy was as quiet and reserved as Fiona was as cheerful and outgoing. While Fiona was a ray of sunshine, Amy was like moonlight. One was bright and the other was soothing; they complemented each other perfectly and got along famously. Possessed of a low, musical voice and a tinkling laugh, Amy had a pleasant personality, which put people at ease. At the seminary, she constantly helped to keep Fiona out of scrapes and helped her attend to her studies. Fiona on her side had helped Amy make friends and settle down and have fun.

Amy was like the sister that Fiona had never known, and her arrival made Fiona happier than she had been in weeks. Soon after Amy had cast off her bonnet and pelisse and tea had been brought to the parlor, the two girls settled on the settee for a comfortable coze. With their feet tucked under them like little girls, they made a pretty picture as they regaled each other with their stories of the time spent apart. Their laughter rang out many times, and the evening sped past.

Amy, however, was not taken in by Fiona's appearance of carefree girlhood. She sensed that there was something troubling her friend, and in her own way she set about coaxing it out of her.

"How is the ton these days? Have you met anyone interesting?"

"Oh! It is a lot of fun. There are endless parties and dances, and everyone attends in all their finery. Now that you are here, you can go with me to all the parties."

"That would be delightful, Fiona. It would be great fun to see how the other debutantes measure up this year. I know that none of them are even close to you in looks. Even in Bath the news of your many successes and suitors have reached my ears. So, tell me, is there a special beau who has captivated your heart?"

Fiona blushed and would not meet her friend's eyes but just shook her head mutely.

"Come on, Fi, out with it! Who is this lad who has been worthy of your attentions? Is he a Corinthian, or a dandy? Is he well-heeled, or is he titled?"

"Yes, I mean no. He is titled, but he is neither a dandy nor a Corinthian, and he most certainly is not a lad."

"Who is this gentleman? Do I know him? Come, dear girl, give me a name. I will not have these secrets between us."

"His name is Philip . . . I mean, Lord Sheffield." Fiona saw the consternation in her friend's face before she could hide it and knew that Philip's reputation was known in Bath as well.

"Tell me the whole story, Fiona, and start at the beginning, for I cannot see how your path should ever have crossed his."

So, Fiona told her the whole story. She didn't leave any of it out. Whatever Amy may have thought about her friend's impulsive behavior she didn't say until the whole convoluted narrative was done. The long-winded story was much interspersed with exclamations and questions. By the end of it, Fiona was in her friend's arms, sobbing her heart out.

"Oh! I hate the wretched man," she said between sobs. "I wished I had never met him."

"There, there, my pet. It's all right now. I can see why you are distressed. He sounds a perfect ogre," Amy said, patting her friend consolingly.

"No, he isn't an ogre, he is actually a kind and honorable man." Fiona fired up at once. "He is nothing like he is rumored to be. He was the perfect gentleman the entire time I stayed at his house."

"But I thought you said he grabbed you and kissed you," Amy asked, confused. "After you had that terrible time getting lost in the mist, no less."

"Yes. But that's only because I slapped him, and he was angry with me for getting lost."

"What about the second time? That time he kissed you after your brother challenged him to a duel. That is truly shameful! I guess rumor speaks truly about him."

"He did no such thing! It was I who kissed him to try to persuade him not to duel with Ted. You are a goose, Amelia Arlington, to listen to gossip!" Fiona cried contradictorily.

"You never did, Fiona Cavendish!" Amy said with an incredulous laugh. "What a naughty minx you have become! Whatever will your brother say if he found out?"

Fiona just sniffed, too overcome to respond.

"If you are not upset over his kiss, then tell me what can possibly be upsetting you now that he is gone?"

"Amy! You do not understand. He stayed in our home for several days, and I devoted my energies to nursing him to health and making sure his days were not dreary. No sooner did the doctor pronounce him fit than the wretched man left without even saying goodbye! He sent a polite note to Ted apologizing for the trouble he caused and thanking the household staff for their care. He even sent Mrs. Kibble flowers, but there was not a word to me. Do you not think that was the most ill-mannered thing you ever heard?"

"Maybe he is a boor and doesn't have any manners?" Amy proposed hesitantly, and her friend turned on her at once.

"You take that back at once, Amy! How could you say so when he exhibited the most perfect manners?"

"Fiona, dear, you are certainly in a contradictory mood. Don't be cross with me, dear one. I will accept that your Lord Sheffield is a paragon of virtue while also being the most aggravating and obtuse man to have upset you so. Let's talk about something else. What do you plan to wear to the Langton ball? Will you permit me to see your gown?" Secretly pleased at Philip being referred to as *her* Lord Sheffield, Fiona allowed herself to be distracted and accompanied Amy amicably to see her new ball gown.

CHAPTER SEVENTEEN

While his sister was thus happily occupied with her bosom friend, Ted had thrown himself into his much-neglected affairs. His health still on the mend from the battle wound and again strained by the duel, he preferred to remain at Red Oaks. Part of the reason for this was also to avoid unnecessary inquiries to prevent his sister's recent escapade from becoming the subject of gossip. However, as his man of affairs, Seldon, was in London, and the state of his affairs at the hands of the honorable Harry Albrighton was bewildering, to say the least, he had to make frequent trips to that gentleman's offices.

On one such occasion, he had the misfortune to meet with an accident. He was returning from London late at night when one of the wheels of his post chaise had come off. The carriage had landed in a ditch, and Ted had been thrown out. Landing on his injured shoulder, he had briefly blacked out. When he had regained consciousness, his man, Bates, who had accompanied him, had helped him out of the ditch. Ted and Bates had unhitched and ridden the horses to the next town to hire another conveyance and make arrangements for the damaged carriage to be repaired. After a delay of several hours, they had made it back to Red Oaks, where a worried Fiona had fussed over Ted and forced him to rest. The debilitating pain had made him stay in bed for a few days, and, truth be told, he quite welcomed the respite.

The presence of Amy in the household was a blessing. When Fiona had first mentioned her friend's visit, Ted had vaguely pictured the scrawny brunette who would come home with his sister during the holidays. He recalled that she had been almost like an orphan to be passed from relative to relative during school breaks. Having lost her own mother at a young age, Fiona had immediately formed a deep bond and kinship with her and had brought her home with her. Amy's father, Colonel Arlington, while from a noble family, was mostly absent from his daughter's life. For some reason, this had set Cousin Sadie against Amy, and she had not thought Amy's other relatives as suitable company for Fiona and had not allowed Fiona to visit her friend. Ted was glad that Fiona had invited her friend for a long, overdue visit.

However, he had not been prepared for her transformation into a beautiful young lady. When Fiona had first introduced Amy to him, her elegant and simple appearance had sparked his admiration immediately. He found her presence soothing after all the simpering debutantes he had encountered while squiring Fiona to various engagements. And he was especially happy for the distraction that Miss Arlington presented. She was just the right influence for his sister, and he hoped that she would divert Fiona's mind off Sheffield. He hoped that she would forget Philip and choose another suitor to marry and therefore present a solution to his worries. He had even considered talking to Amy about it but had thought that might be too forward and desisted from the impulse. Meanwhile, he was content to see the two of them busy shopping and attending parties and to see his sister laughing and enjoying herself while he convalesced.

His convalescence, however, was interrupted when Harry Albrighton came to solicit after his health. Ted lost no time in raking his heir over the coals over his expenses during Ted's absence. "How you can manage to spend five thousand pounds in a year, I cannot imagine," he said, his eyes glinting with anger.

"I had to keep up appearances, Cousin," Harry Albrighton said in his placating tones, which infuriated Ted further.

"You mean you have rigged yourself as a dandy and also been hitting the gambling tables hard. It's a good thing I returned before your 'appearances' sent us all to ruin, Cousin," Ted bit out. "From now on, you will exercise moderation and live within your allowance."

"Cousin Ted, surely you cannot mean that?" Harry's smile wavered as alarm and something akin to malice crossed fleetingly into his eyes, making Ted blink in surprise. When he stared at Harry questioningly, his cousin's face had assumed his habitual oily expression, and he was back to his annoyingly self-effacing manner. "I mean, Cousin, that's a bit harsh. After all I have done for Fiona and to keep your affairs running smoothly in your absence."

"I do mean it, Albrighton. I will go so far as to pay your present creditors, but I will have your word that there will be no more of them. My own affairs are far from smooth. In fact, the tenants at Red Oaks have many complaints regarding our treatment of them. You have also needlessly worried Fiona and tried to force her into marriage. These are hardly recommendations in your favor."

"Ted, you know I hold Fiona in the highest admiration and esteem. I would never deliberately cause her distress. When I received no word about your state, I assumed the worst. I thought by marrying Fiona I could give her my name and protect her from fortune hunters. Also, it seemed a most amiable solution, as it would allow her to remain in her ancestral home and with her loving family."

"The loving family that forced her to flee, you mean?' Ted's voice was very chill, and his gaze turned decidedly frosty.

"I am not sure why Cousin Fiona chose to leave us so abruptly. If there was anything not to her liking, she had only to mention it for me to set it right. Her every wish is my command, and that is why I seek your permission to ask for her hand in marriage."

Ted's gaze turned to ice chips. "I cannot grant it, Albrighton. You have made a mull of things in my absence and turned Fiona against you. I will never force my sister into marriage with anyone. So, let's not speak of this again. Now, do I have your word that you will stay away from gambling dens for a while?"

Ted's tone brooked no argument, and Harry Albrighton, however churlishly, had no choice but to give his word that he would keep away from the gambling dens and slink away. When he had gone, Ted breathed a sigh of relief. He had feared that Albrighton would continue to press his suit for Fiona's hand and become an annoyance. He hoped he had succeeded in diverting that scheme.

CHAPTER EIGHTEEN

It was no use trying to immerse himself in his estate affairs. Philip ran a weary hand through his hair and sighed deeply. Every time he looked at his books, a pale face with enormous, green eyes floated in front of him, looking at him with hurt and contempt. He had only himself to blame, of course. It had been his intent to make her despise him and forget him, and it appeared that he had succeeded all too well. If looks could kill, he would have perished in the Langton gardens that day. As it was, he was left to wallow in guilt for his deeds.

When he had left Red Oaks a fortnight ago, he had naïvely imagined that putting distance between them would take care of his attraction to Fiona. That she would fade from his memory, and he could go back to the way things had been before she had burst into his life like a firecracker, blazing, a trail of light and beauty in her wake. He had tried to immerse himself in his work but to no avail. His thoughts, despite all his efforts, had persisted on dwelling worshipfully on the green-eyed, fiery-haired goddess. He could not even pass the pianoforte without remembering the precious minutes they had spent at it in perfect harmony and accord. How he wished he could have stopped time at that moment so he could relive it over and over again.

No matter how much he tried to deny it, he had finally come to the unfortunate conclusion that in the matter of Miss Fiona Cavendish, his feelings had become well and truly engaged. Judging by Fiona's concern over his well-being during his unwilling sojourn at Red Oaks, he suspected that his feelings were reciprocated. This awareness in any normal, red-blooded man would have incited joy and the will to gain her hand by all means. It only filled Philip with dread. He had, through his own stubbornness, earned a reputation that prevented him from marrying any wellborn female. Any lady he married would instantly be tarred by the same brush of scandal that had painted him the veriest black since Elizabeth had met her untimely demise. Just the thought of that innocent girl being shamed on his account made his blood boil. Philip, therefore, came to the conclusion that he could not offer for Fiona no matter how much he longed to do so. He had to forget her.

Even his best intentions were no match for the influence she had on his heart, however. He had resorted to drink, his trusted companion in hard times, but even that had brought no solace. He missed her so much that it hurt. Finally impatient at his own foolishness, he acknowledged that drastic measures were called for. This would never do. There was nothing except heartbreak down that path. His last conversation with Ted had made it clear that Ted believed the rumors that surrounded his unfortunate marriage, and therefore he could not in honor pursue Fiona. His own feelings were of no consequence; he was a man in charge of his life and could continue his life, however dismal, by ignoring them. Fiona was a different matter. He could not allow her to hope, as that would prevent her from accepting another man as her husband. She was too young to have her heart broken; she had to be made to see the error of his ways. He had to somehow make her despise him and forget about him. What was a man of honor to do when he found himself in the horns of a dilemma? Turn to deception, of course!

Philip, despite rumors, had never been much in the petticoat line. His brief marriage had turned him off romance, though many a willing lady had set her cap at him. Not being a monk, he had occasionally indulged in the company of a willing widow or two, but even these liaisons were few and far between, as he did not condescend to be part of the London scene or opera circuit too often. However, he knew enough about women to understand that nothing enraged them more than a man giving his attention to another female. Unfortunately, none of these ladies of his previous dalliances would suit for his plan to disillusion the innocent Miss Fiona Cavendish.

As he had stared despondently at his invitation to the Langton ball that had arrived in the morning mail, he slumped, dejected, seeing no solution to his problem. He had brushed the invitation away impatiently when his eye alighted on a letter penned with a feminine hand and wafting the scent of rose essence. The letter was from Lady Anne Carson.

Lady Anne was notoriously known to be a widow of means, who did as she pleased, thumbing her nose to the ton. She cared little for convention and did not accept invitations to the various entertainments that the season afforded. Instead, she set herself up as an artist, accepting commissions where she chose. Being talented, her skill was much in demand, but she turned down several aristocrats to accept small commissions in the country that took her away from the London scene. Philip had encountered this delightful lady at a dinner given by Hector Bainbridge not long before his encounter with Fiona. He had found her both charming and knowledgeable, not to mention easy on the eyes. He had spent several delightful hours in the lady's company, and a great friendship had been formed. They had soon been on a first-name basis, each having assured the other that they had no designs other than a platonic comradeship.

Lady Anne had mentioned that she wished to visit him at Crossfields to do a landscape in oils of the magnificent house and estate. Her tinkling laugh had rung out when he had mentioned that he was a bachelor domicile and that she should come suitably chaperoned. "Neither of our reputations can suffer more than they already have, Phil, don't you think? We must do as we choose, and if I choose to stay at your home unchaperoned, then propriety be damned," she had stated gaily.

Now reading her letter, Philip smiled, recalling that exchange, and knew he had his solution. The time was right to capture the beauty and glory of the gardens in summer on canvas. And with her in residence, he could hope to disenchant Fiona from whatever feelings she was harboring toward him.

Thus it was that his scheme had been born, and if he had his way, it would solve all his problems. His innocent flirtation with Lady Anne, coupled with the wagging tongues of the gossips who witnessed it at the Langton ball, would put out the eager light in Fiona's eyes. She would hate him and probably accept the hand of someone more worthy, like Hector, and thereby be out of his reach, and he could put the whole thing behind him. The thought did little to elevate his spirits. Nothing could change his feelings for her, he acknowledged to himself ruefully.

CHAPTER NINETEEN

On the day of the ball, Fiona was tempted to plead a headache and not go. Then her usual common sense took over, and she decided she would not let one cynical rake affect her own behavior. She would show him that he did not intimidate her. She dressed for the ball with great care. Her new gown of ivory lace trimmed with emerald satin was very becoming. Marcie had exerted considerable effort in getting her dressed, and when she had finished, Fiona looked enchantingly beautiful. Amy was a perfect complement to her in a pale-blue-and-primrose silk gown, and Fiona had noted how Ted's eyes turned from startled surprise to admiration when he had perceived Amy, and she had been secretly delighted. When the two girls arrived at the Langton ball, one on each of Ted's arms, all eyes seemed to turn to them, and there was a lull in the conversation. By the time they were done with the reception line, young men tripped over themselves in trying to get to their side. Both their dance cards were soon full, as some of the most eligible bachelors in attendance vied for their attention.

Fiona acknowledged that she was the envy of every other hopeful young lady present. Every matron with a less spectacular-looking daughter was annoyed with her. After enduring life with her cousins, she welcomed the change of scene and gaiety, and secretly hoped that her meeting with Philip would have the desired results. Even her cousin Harry claiming a dance did not dim her smile as she dreamed about their prospective encounter. While she positively glowed under all the attention, her eyes roved the ballroom, seeking out one tall, dark figure, and was disappointed, for he wasn't there. As the evening progressed, she couldn't help but feel anticlimactic as he did not appear. How typical! She thought, anger fueling her disappointment, and her enjoyment of the festivities started to ebb. However, knowing that many eyes were on her, she put on a brave face as she resolved to have a great time and enjoy herself.

She greeted her many friends and introduced Amy to them and endured the attention of her many flattering beaux. The time ticked on slowly. Much later, in between dances, she was in the middle of mild flirtation with Hector Bainbridge when she noticed a hush fall around her as the conversations stilled. All eyes had turned to look at a pair of new arrivals. And there he was dressed in black and silver with a strikingly beautiful, blonde lady dressed boldly in peacock blue clinging to his arm. Philip's eyes seemed to pierce hers across the ballroom, and for minute Fiona felt breathless as she held his gaze, oblivious of all else. It seemed to her that all around her had faded away except him, and that the two of them were enveloped in a magical moment all their own. Then Philip turned away to talk to his host, and the moment was broken.

As Philip advanced into the ballroom, a path seemed to clear in front of him, as more people turned away and acted busy rather than acknowledge him. Several gentlemen glared at him through their quizzing glasses as he passed. However, Fiona noticed there was also much interest in him from many simpering debutantes and their mamas, who were apparently prepared to forgive anything for his title. Hector saw him approach and hailed his friend. Philip joined them, bringing the lady with him. He bowed politely to Fiona, shook Hector's hand, and introduced his companion as Lady Anne Carson. Lady Anne, whose shimmering silk gown was most striking, and also very décolleté and showed off her charms to advantage, returned Fiona's curtsy and then clung to Philip's arm in a proprietary manner, or so it appeared to Fiona.

"It's good to see you back on your feet, Phil," said Hector, alluding to Philip's recent injury.

"It was a mere scratch that has been much fussed over," Philip responded, his voice dripping with boredom. Fiona felt slighted, though his remark was not directed at her, and her mood deteriorated further. The spark that had erupted when she had first seen him enter fizzled and died, and she felt drained.

The band struck up the next dance just then, and Lord Hector bowed to Fiona saying, "It's my waltz, I believe, Miss Cavendish."

Fiona bestowed him with a brilliant, albeit fake, smile and offered her gloved hand so he could lead her into the German dance that was all the rage. Philip bowed to Lady Anne and led her onto the dance floor. As Fiona twirled around in the arms of her partner, her eyes followed Philip and his beautiful partner, who gracefully waltzed nearby, deep in what appeared to be an intimate conversation. She was hard-pressed to keep up her end of the requisite polite conversation without missing a step. She feared to acknowledge what she saw, for it spelled an end to her own hopes and dreams. So, she tried not to think and instead focused on Hector's conversation and allowing his open admiration to soothe her ruffled feathers.

For the remainder of the night, Fiona was kept busy going from one dance partner to another, or she was having a conversation with one or other of her gentlemen admirers seeking her attention. But no matter where she was or whom she was with, it was hard to not notice the striking couple in their midst: the tall figure in black and silver, paying court to the sophisticated blonde beauty. Every time she danced, with a solicitous partner, her eyes sought them out. She observed him holding Lady Anne close, closer than needed, if truth be told, and whispering into her ears and making her laugh. The sight and sound made her feel ill, and she had no appetite for the carefully selected hors d'oeuvre that her beaux plied her with. By the time Harry Albrighton came to claim his dance, she had a pounding headache, and she begged him to walk with her outside instead so that she may get some fresh air.

Outside, Harry murmured effusive compliments that only nauseated her further, and he attempted to hold her hand. He followed that with plaintive entreaties that he was heartbroken she had not accepted his offer. Fiona listened to him politely, but retrieving her hand, said that while she was flattered by his devotion, she was resolved to only marry for love. At that moment, they heard a laugh coming from behind a bush some yards away and then the blonde beauty darted out, looking behind her and laughing as she made her way inside. She was followed by Philip, who strolled leisurely back to the house. Realizing that she had witnessed a rendezvous, Fiona's heart plummeted all the way to her feet, and she turned to see Albrighton watching her speculatively.

"It's only Sheffield and his lady friend," Harry said, stating the obvious. "Why, coz? Are you unwell? You have turned as pale as if you had seen a ghost. I wish your innocent eyes had not seen that lecher in action, but don't let it ruin your evening."

"Cousin Harry, I do feel a headache coming on, could we please go back inside so I can rest for a few minutes?" Harry bowed deeply and held her elbow with undue solitude as he escorted her back to the house.

Once inside, she excused herself and went to an anteroom to calm down. Amy found her there and comforted her while she unburdened her much-tried heart of her feelings of anger, disillusionment, and disappointment to her best friend. Amy held her hands and patted them while murmuring soothing phrases until Fiona calmed herself down.

When the girls finally returned to the ballroom, Fiona had fully regained her composure, and she danced and flirted the rest of the evening as expected. To the other guests, she was the belle of the ball. Only Amy and Ted could see past dazzling smile and tinkling laugh and know that she was not happy. While to all appearances she was gay, the brilliant smile on her lips seldom touched her eyes.

When they finally took their leave of their host and returned home, she excused herself to her brother and Amy and went to her room. Once Marcie helped her into her night rail, she dismissed her, but instead of going to bed, she went and sat by the window to stare into the night. She had to accept what she had witnessed with her own eyes. The night had been a revelation in more ways than one. She knew with certainty that what she felt for Philip was love. The deep, true, and enduring kind of love she had always hoped to feel. However, she had to acknowledge that her love was not returned, for she had the misfortune of falling in love with a most undeserving man! The man who had captured her heart was the most notorious rake. Rumors about Philip had spoken truly.

Still, she loved him, for rake though he was, she had seen a crack in his veneer and glimpsed a much different man than what the world had told her he was. A man who had treated her gently and with care, who was beloved by his faithful retainers, who had risked his own life to spare her brother. But why? Today he had shown her that he had no real feelings for her. She had thought he desired her once, but he had been so fickle as to switch his affections to another so soon. That she had been just one of his many flirtations had been made abundantly clear tonight. He had brought his latest love interest to the ball and had not so much as said a word to Fiona. What a tiresome man he was!

She knew now that she had loved him from the first, but it had taken the sharp pang of anguish and jealousy when she had seen him with another woman to make her understand her own feelings. She acknowledged sadly that she loved him whether he loved her or not. He remained beyond her reach, yet she would love him forever. No matter what the world thought of him, to her he would be her first love.

She recalled with sadness how the tongues had wagged that night about him. How many slurs were cast on him. He had borne it all without appearing to be affected by any of it. And she couldn't help but admire his fortitude. Yes, she had fallen in love, but with the wrong man, and now she was lost. There was certainly no hope that he would love her in return. She was doomed to a life of loving him from afar and unable to marry anyone else.

Feeling as she did about him, her code of honor forbade her from accepting any other man. She knew Hector only needed the slightest encouragement to offer for her. He was a fine man, and worthy, and Ted held him in great esteem. They would suit, but she could never love him as she loved Philip. And that was not fair to Hector. Her birthday was coming up fast, and her chance at having an independent life would be lost with her youth. It was price she was willing to pay. She had once dreamed of using her wealth to set up a school for orphans and girls from poor surroundings. Ted may still allow her to pursue this in some way if it were his choice, but he would marry one day, and his future wife and family would need to be considered. She had to resign herself to the life of a dependent spinster. She deserved it for her hoydenish starts and for falling in love with a heartless but lovable rake.

CHAPTER TWENTY

Marcie Hinckley had availed her day off to go to town. Miss Fiona had some shopping to be done, and Marcie had volunteered to do them before her visit to her "Uncle Sam." Jim Coachman had some errands to complete for Master Ted, and so the coach had brought Marcie to town in style. She had quickly completed her errands and then, arranging a time and place to meet up with Joe Coachman later, went off on her own. But instead of going to meet the fictional uncle, she went to an out-of-the-way coffee shop, where a young man was anxiously awaiting her arrival at a worn-out table with two rickety chairs.

"Marcie, my girl, it's good to see you," said Samuels, Philip's valet, for it was none other.

"It's good to see you again, Mr. Samuels," said Marcie demurely. She glanced around nervously before seating herself at the table. Samuels sat down beside her.

"Is that a new bonnet? You look mighty fetching, if I may say so," Samuels said with an appreciative grin.

"Yes, thank you." Marcie blushed.

"It's been a while since I've seen you, and it's been hard on me," Samuels said glumly.

"It's only going to get worse," Marcie said and then turned to request a pot of tea and some buns from the girl wearing a much-darned skirt and apron who appeared, surly-faced, to take their order.

"He has been worse than a bear with a sore head." Samuels shook his head and sighed. "It's hard to get away."

"She won't even hear his name." Marcie let out a great big sigh.

"Now that Miss Amy has returned to Bath, she is lonelier than ever, poor soul. Even Sir Ted cannot coax a smile out of her, and he does try, poor man."

"Well, what shall we do? It looks like there is no hope that he will court her." Samuels sounded depressed.

"If they don't get hitched, then there is no hope for us neither," stated Marcie dolefully.

Their tea arrived and was plonked on the table with such force, almost making it totter. The girl disappeared without a word, and Marcie poured the tea for them both.

"You could always leave your situation and find another. Mayhap I can ask Mrs. Pork to find you something in our household," suggested Samuels as he took a gulp of the lukewarm, mud-colored fluid in his chipped cup.

"I would never leave my mistress, especially not when she is down in the boughs like she is now. You may want to apply for a post with Sir Ted instead," Marcie replied with alacrity. She took a dainty sip and grimaced, then added a few more spoonfuls of sugar to her cup.

Samuels shook his head. "Me and Lord Sheffield, we go ways back. My master will be lost without me," he said.

They both gave a collective sigh and sipped dismally. The future looked bleak to both of them, and they looked at each other sadly, unable to see their way out.

"It would be good if there were some ways to force their hand," Marcie said slowly.

"I've been thinking the same thing," cried Samuels excitedly. "And maybe there is."

"Are you thinking what I'm thinking?" asked Marcie.

"If you are thinking that it would be unfortunate if the word should get out that Miss Cavendish was alone and unchaperoned at Lord Sheffield's house for the better part of a week, then yes, I agree."

Marcie nodded assent. "I would never drag my mistress's name through muck," she said ruefully, "but that horrid Mr. Harry has been nosing about and asking all kinds of questions at the stables, and I fear he has guessed what exactly happened when Miss Fiona ran way. So, what's to say but that he may well let the truth slip out accidentally, if you know what I mean." Marcie tapped her nose meaningfully.

"As it happens, a little bird in the household told me that the ne'er-do-well cousin of Sir Ted's has already been dropping hints about the affair. Nothin' that can be traced back to the source, mind, and nothin' but bits and pieces. But enough to create rumor and what the nobs would call juicy gossip."

"Oh my word! My poor lady! What does his lordship think of this gossip?"

"The poor man has immersed himself in his estate and doesn't know the nasty things being said about them. But if news were to reach him, then he will offer for her, I am sure of it! He is a man of honor, and he will do the right thing rather than allow a lady's name to be dragged through the mud. His first wife's death was rough on his lordship, and he done sworn off marriage forever. But if he thinks that she's been ruined 'cause of him, he'll offer for her, mark my words! For he is a true-blue bloke, my guv'nor, that he is!" said Samuels confidently.

"If he doesn't offer, then Sir Ted is sure to call him out, and we don't want that," said Marcie doubtfully.

"No! That we don't," he agreed. "He barely survived the last duel. Don't worry m' girl, it won't come to that. I happen to know that he is pining for her. He is just too stubborn to admit it."

"And she loves him too. Only he has made her mad by setting up a flirtation with that blonde lady painter, and she refuses to forgive him." Marcie sighed.

"There you are then, my gel. It's a 'forlorm cityeshun,' as my master would say."

"Word of the duel, too, has already reached the ton, except no one knows why they fought, as both Lord Sheffield and Sir Ted, and their respective friends, have been awfully closemouthed about it," Marcie acceded slowly.

"Then, it's decided. We just need to drop the tale into a few choice ears that have big mouths attached and wait."

"Will the nobs believe the story?" Marcie twisted her hands in distress. "Miss Fiona is such a gentle soul and already sunken in despair. All the joy has left her, scandal may well send her into a decline."

"Oh! Pish! Your mistress ain't no wilting flower. She got fire, that one! She will not stand to be insulted. She is a fighter, mark my words. And besides, what other choice do we have? It's either this or one of us has to look for other employment, and neither of us wants to do that. Besides, rumors of your mistress staying at his house have already hit the neighboring villages. They just don't know her name, so all some busybody needs to do is furnish that and leave the rest to the waggin' tongues. The fat is bound to hit the fire soon, we might as well move it along apace."

Marcie nodded but still looked a bit unconvinced, so he continued.

"They will believe anything bad about my master. Ever since her ladyship fell to her death, the ton gossips have been painting him with a tarred brush at the slightest provocation. Now there's been the duel. If people hear that the duel was caused because of Miss Cavendish, it will ring true."

"Very well. It's settled, then. Let's get to work. If all goes well, the whole ton should be buzzing with scandal by this time tomorrow." With a sad smile, Marcie took leave of her beau and went off to meet the coach to take her home.

CHAPTER TWENTY-ONE

Ted was livid with rage. On his most recent visit to the city, he had deigned to make an appearance at White's. It was at this esteemed institution that he had heard his sister's name bandied about, and he was offered much commiseration. Thinking that the duel had ignited the rumors, he had initially blamed himself. The gossip had succeeded in returning to many minds—and tongues—the memories of the previous scandal in Sheffield's life. For Ted, they reignited the painful memories buried in his own heart. Determined not to do anything brash until the rumors blew over, he had returned to Red Oaks. He had given Fiona a semblance of the situation so she may not be taken unawares by the tide of tattle. He had not counted on the concocted stories she heard from the many visiting busybodies who signed over tea in false sympathy, which only served to enrage Ted further. He wished dearly that his sister's friend, Amy, had remained with them to comfort Fiona. He even considered sending Fiona to Bath until the whole thing had died down, but she refused to run and hide, for it would only give truth to the falsehoods.

Ted, therefore, closeted himself in his study trying to focus on his estate and gave his staff strict instructions that he was not to be disturbed. His intent in avoiding the whole situation was thwarted by Harry Albrighton. That interfering personage had burst into his study and launched a tirade against Philip Merton. Edward had then learned from Albrighton that the rumors had been traced back to Sheffield. In a burst of outrage, Ted had saddled his mount and ridden out like a tempest.

CHAPTER TWENTY-TWO

Philip Merton was sitting at his desk attending his correspondence. His eyes were on it, but his mind remained focused on a red-headed angel who had watched over him while he recovered. What was she doing right now? Probably riding with one of her friends or out about town. How he wished he could be the one escorting her. He shook his head, angry with himself for indulging in a fantasy that would never be. He was not a green lad, but a grown man of eight and twenty. It was not as if he loved her, for he was incapable of ever loving again. His heart was closed off forever, for only a fool would make the same mistake twice. The minx had been a passing infatuation, and that because he had been so lonely. He sighed heavily and returned to his ledger.

The door opened "Mr. Edward Cavendish." Moseley announced.

Philip looked up in surprise, for once forgetting to look bored. He rose to his feet as Edward rushed in.

"You scoundrel!" he shouted, and giving Philip no chance to react, grabbed him by the collar. "Just because she refused your attentions and you lost our duel, did you have to be a complete cad and smear her reputation?"

"I have no idea what drivel it is you speak of, Cavendish." Philip disengaged himself from Ted's grasp.

He walked over to the brandy decanter and poured them both a drink. "State your accusations calmly, man, if you can pull yourself together," he told Ted, handing him a glass.

Ted tossed back the drink, and setting the glass down, he glowered at Philip. "I am talking about your bandying my sister's name around.

Rumors of her running away and staying at your house and our duel are now circulating the ton. Everywhere there are wild whispers that you kidnapped and molested her and took her virtue by force. Our duel is attributed to my trying to avenge our honor. Word is, angry at losing the duel, you have tried to besmirch Fiona's name."

Philip paled perceptibly on hearing this. "Ted, I swear, I have not breathed a word to anyone about our duel and certainly not about your sister. Even Bainbridge and Langton do not know all the reasons of why we fought."

"It was your servants, then," Cavendish bit out.

"My servants are loyal to me and would not have done such a thing." Philip's voice rose with displeasure.

"Maybe it is their ill-conceived loyalty to you that made them slur Fiona's name."

"Anyone in my employ knows better than to do that. I swear on my honor that I do not know who could have done this." His chill tone barely hid his affront to the implied accusation.

"Why should I accept your word? If all that is said about you is true, then you are no gentleman and have no honor," Ted said blisteringly.

"You may believe whatever you choose. And if my word is not enough for you, I will meet you again to clear my name."

"I would call you out again if I thought it would serve any purpose. But it will only make the tongues wag faster."

"What do you intend to do?"

"Dammed if I know. What a farce this is becoming! When I find out who is behind this, I will kill him." Ted glared at Philip.

"How is Fio . . . your sister taking this?" Philip inquired softly.

"As well as can be expected. She is confined to Red Oaks but puts on a brave face and will not hide from the tabbies who come to visit trying to pry for information. My cousin Sadie is staying with us to lend support, and my cousin Harry has offered to marry her to quiet the wagging tongues."

"Harry Albrighton? That milquetoast!" Philip spat the name out in disgust. "Surely you are not considering him as a suitor for your sister?"

Ted almost forgot his chagrin and grinned at this untoward display of displeasure before saying, "I am at point nonplussed with the whole situation. Fiona has always dreamed of marrying for love, and I have encouraged her to believe that she will find the man of her dreams. But now with her reputation in shreds, she will have little chance of a suitable offer. And time is running out. If she does not marry soon, she will forfeit her inheritance and her independence. I do not want my sister to end up a bitter spinster nor have to depend on any man for her allowance for the rest of her life."

Philip did not look up or respond for a few minutes. When he finally looked up, his eyes were uncertain, serious even, but his expression was far from cynical. "Cavendish, as I am the apparent villain in this piece, I should perhaps be the one to make amends. I hope you will permit me to set this right by offering for her. My prospects are certainly better than those of Albrighton, he's known to frequent the gaming tables besides being pockets to let," he said simply.

Ted walked to the window and stared out in silence. When he finally spoke, he sounded troubled. "I do not mean to insult you, Sheffield, but while you certainly have a lot to offer Fiona, I am not convinced that being married to a man with your reputation will bring her any happiness. You live the life of a recluse in the country. She is a vivacious young woman with a vibrant personality and a love of life. I will not have her shut away here because you choose to hide away from scandalmongers. Not that I blame you for it. I would do the same if I had to quell wagging tongues every time I stepped foot in the capital. Yet wag they will, for some still hold you guilty of abusing Elizabeth and causing her death."

Philip cursed loudly. "Damn you, Ted! We were friends once, and yet you always choose to believe the worst of me. You did so five years ago, and you are doing so again. You were mistaken then as you are now. I no more abused my wife than I mauled your sister," he said.

"I never believed the rumors but rather saw the evidence of bruises on her with my own eyes. If you recall, I asked you for the truth then and again more recently, but you consistently refuse to provide an explanation. So, what should I have believed?" Ted demanded.

"You should have trusted me!" Philip responded hotly.

"If you are innocent of all blame, then why will you not defend yourself?" Ted shouted.

"Because a gentleman does not speak ill of a lady, especially when the lady was my own wife. And whether you believe it or not, I have always adhered to the code of conduct required from a gentleman." Philip spoke earnestly and with a firmness that lent truth to his word.

Ted looked nonplussed. "It is ultimately Fiona's decision. She has strong convictions about love and may not choose to marry just to prevent scandal," he said thoughtfully.

"Love!" Philip scoffed. "There is no such thing. You will do better to disabuse your sister from such notions. I can only offer her respect, anything more is delusion. I am too old for love in any case."

"You are only twenty-eight years old, as am I. Hardly an old man."

"Maybe not in years, but my heart is old and withered. I loved once and lost, and I do not care to repeat the experience. I will never love again." Philip's mouth twisted in a cynical sneer.

"Spare me your woes! If you think that life has been cruel to you, how much worse is a life in which your love is forever denied?" Ted spoke quietly, almost to himself. "Do you know how much it hurts when you long for your love and see her with another? Would you rather have had such a life in which you had no hope?"

Philip stared at Ted, nonplussed. Finally, he walked over to him and grabbed him by the shoulders.

"Ted. I don't believe this. You fool! You are still in love with Elizabeth and breaking your heart over her, aren't you?" he demanded. Ted looked away and did not respond. Philip sighed and moved to stand by the mantelpiece, staring into the fire broodingly. When he spoke next, his voice was controlled but charged with emotion.

"I am going to go against my own code of honor and tell you something that I haven't divulged to another soul till now. I want to lay some ghosts to rest so that we can both move on with our lives. Do I have your word that you will never repeat it? For if you do, I will deny all of it."

Receiving a nod from Ted, Philip poured them both another drink and tossed his back in gulp, then spoke in an emotionless voice. "I loved Elizabeth from the first moment I saw her. I thought her the dearest, purest, and most beautiful woman in the world. I knew you were hurt when she chose me over you, but I was too in love to care. I like to think that she loved me too, at least at first. My mistake was to believe that she would be content to live in the country with me. A few months into our marriage, she became restless. She did not like life in the country with its limited entertainment. She grew bored with the company she kept and missed her friends in the ton and its parties and festivities. She was so unhappy that I sent her to her cousin in London for an extended visit. She was delighted, and she wrote frequently at first, saying how much fun she was having.

"As months went by, I asked her to return to me, but she kept putting it off, and I was busy with the estate. My father was ailing, and his estate needed attending, so there was much for me to do. My presence was needed here. But her letters became less frequent, and something about them caused me disquiet. I made the journey to London, hoping to persuade her to come back with me." Philip paused in his narrative to pour himself another drink, and his hands shook, slopping the amber liquid onto the rich carpet. He took a big swallow before resuming.

"Elizabeth was not happy to see me, and she refused to even consider returning to Crossfields. Every time I tried to reason with her, she would burst into tears and run sobbing from the room. So much so that her cousin's household believed I was abusing her. I believe now that she even self-inflicted some bruises on herself to give credence to the story. The servants' tales gave grist to the rumor mills, and people would whisper wherever I went. It got to me, and I yearned to leave it all and return home but was resolved not to leave without her."

Philip choked with emotion, and his voice faltered. He stared at the fire for a few minutes before he continued. "On that fateful day, everything came to a climax. I had received word that my father had taken a turn for the worse. I begged and pleaded with Elizabeth that morning to leave it all behind and go home with me, but she laughed and said that the ton loved her and hated me. She said that she no longer loved me but loved another and carried his child. She was going to leave me, she said, so the portion of my fortune which was not entailed would go to her. She said she would kill me and claim that I had tried to kill her. Everyone would believe that she had shot me in self-defense. I was shattered beyond reason by her betrayal and tried to wrest the gun from her, but it went off and hit me in my shoulder. Elizabeth was scared that I would stop her and screamed and ran for the stairs, calling for the servants to help her. I called out to her to stop, but she slipped and fell down the stairs to her death.

"I was laid up in bed for a fortnight, and when I finally recovered,

I had already been condemned by my peers with my reputation as a wife abuser and murderer firmly established. The press claimed she had tried to shoot me out of fear, and then I had pushed her to her death. Bow Street looked into it but couldn't prove anything. I was heartsick with grief and misery and did not even defend myself. Then, a few days later, you confronted me saying that I was a wife killer, and it was the last straw that my own best friend should turn against me. I was angry, and I thought you might have been her lover, and I wanted to fight you just to end those rumors once and for all. So, I hit you. You challenged, and I chose pistols because I knew your prowess with the sword. By the time of the duel, I had calmed down and knew you could not have been so dishonorable, so I meant to merely hit you on the arm, but you moved at the last instant and were severely injured. The ton turned our duel into a farce. After that, the newspapers had a field day with large editorials about the poor, abused lady with the wicked husband who had tried to kill her only champion. I was sick of it all by then. I did not want any more scandal, so I just accepted my fate as an outcast and have remained one since." Philip leaned against the fireplace as if recounting the tragedy had drained him. He looked at Ted questioningly.

Ted stared back at him, his face reflecting such horror and disillusionment that Philip's hope that his word had been believed was rekindled. Ted at last knew the truth about the woman to whom he had pledged his loyalty.

A few moments passed in silence as each man reflected on his folly. It was Ted who first broke the silence. "Did you ever find out who was her lover?" he asked quietly.

Philip shook his head. "I couldn't make inquiries without causing more scandal and making tongues wag even more. So I just let it be. Tell me now, Ted, do you still believe in true love? For I ceased to believe in it the day Elizabeth died."

"I still believe in true love, though it is true both you and I have been unlucky in love till now. But I believe that a love such as my parents experienced must exist," Ted insisted.

Philip smiled his cynical smile and said, "None of this is going to help our situation with Fiona. Will you at least permit that I speak to your sister? I promise you that if she should accept me, I will do my best to keep her happy."

"You may speak to Fiona, but the decision is still hers. If she accepts your hand, then you have my blessing." Ted extended his hand, and Philip clasped it. There was nothing left to be said as a new and tenuous bond was forged between them.

At that moment, the door to the study opened, and Moseley announced Mrs. Carson. The beautiful Anne sashaying into the room, wearing an elegant morning gown of deep-blue satin and with her blonde hair coiled in becoming curls around her expressive face, could not hide her surprise in seeing the earnest tableau they presented.

Philip, summoning up a smile, went forward to take Anne's hand and lead her toward his visitor.

"Cavendish, may I present my esteemed guest, Lady Anne Carson. Lady Anne, Sir Edward Cavendish is an old fr . . . acquaintance," he finished the introductions lamely.

Ted bowed over Lady Anne and said all that was proper. His eyes were alight with curiosity at the beauty's presence at Sheffield's house. Philip, interpreting the glance correctly, explained. "Lady Anne is residing in a cottage on my estate as my honored guest, as she has kindly consented also to exert her considerable talent to capturing the Crossfields summer gardens on canvas."

"I would be greatly honored to see your masterpiece, Lady Anne." Ted managed to hide his surprise and, recovering his composure, smiled charmingly at the lady.

"You will have to be patient, sir. My work has only just begun."

"I will be sure to host a soiree to unveil your completed work for all your admirers to view," Philip stated.

Ted took up his hat and riding crop, bowed to Lady Anne, and, obtaining a promise from her that he should be included in that company, made his departure. When the door had closed behind him, the beauty turned toward her host with a laugh. "Lord, I was sure I had interrupted a quarrel when I entered. You were both so serious."

"Nothing of the kind, my dear lady. Ted was merely paying a morning call."

"Cavendish," Lady Anne said slowly. "Wasn't that the name of the pretty girl we met at the Langton ball?"

"Yes, the Lady Fiona is Ted's sister." Philip sounded almost brusque.

"Philip, my dear friend, I was not born yesterday, and it only took a moment at the ball for me to realize that you have given your heart to the lively Miss Cavendish. So, will you not tell me what ails you? Does Cavendish not support your courtship of his sister? Is that why he was here—to warn you away?"

"I wish it were only that simple. I fear I have made a proper mull of things."

"Not least by striving to make your love jealous by expending all your attention on me at the ball."

"I was trying to warn her off, as I don't see myself as worthy of an innocent like her."

"What fustian you speak, Philip! Now, best come clean and tell me the whole, as I can see that there is more to this tale."

Thus it was that Philip made a clean breast of the whole situation and was mortified to hear Anne's tinkling peal of laughter ring out many times over his botched efforts to drive Fiona away.

"So, what would you have me do, wise one?" he asked, annoyed.

"Go to her and tell how you feel. Ask for her hand, you foolish man," Anne said, smiling at him with genuine affection.

CHAPTER TWENTY-THREE

The next morning, Fiona worked on her embroidery or at least attempted to do so for her thoughts kept wandering, and her work did not progress much at all. Outwardly she appeared calm and cheerful, but inside she was in turmoil. Ever since those nasty rumors had started two days ago, she had known no peace. Her cousin Sadie had shown up bursting with righteous indignation at the insult to her beloved niece. Fiona, who had expected that the truth of her escapade would eventually come out, had borne the news with stoicism.

What she did not expect was the deluge of matrons that descended on Red Oaks, all professing sympathy for the "poor, wronged child" and wondering aloud "whatever would she do now." Advice was offered, lace kerchiefs were plied over dry eyes, and platitudes were uttered in the hope of gleaning more information. Each new visitor brought even more wild stories about how she had been chased and abducted by the villainous Lord Sheffield, who had planned the dastardly deed believing her to be alone and helpless. The stories varied from him grabbing her and tossing her onto his horse and galloping off to her being drugged and bound and tossed into his carriage. Or her entire carriage being abducted at gunpoint. The ladies had shivered and shook their heads in disgust at the more scandalous details of her being molested and being held prisoner until her brother had rescued her. The rumor mill then had it that Edward Cavendish nearly killed Sheffield in a duel.

The stories had enraged Fiona. For some odd reason, she was more concerned about the fact that Philip was being blamed for crimes he had not committed than the damage to her reputation. However, she had valiantly maintained her composure. But when she tried to deny the truth in any of the stories, the ladies of the ton had only clucked with sympathy that the "poor child" was in denial. This only enraged her further. She had borne as much of it as she could until, finally, she had given up and left Cousin Sadie to field the visitors' inquisitive questions.

She had hoped that Ted would not be brash and would wait for it to blow over, and for a while it had seemed he would. However, Cousin Harry had poured fuel on the fire by naming Philip as the villain. After that, nothing would stop Ted from accosting Philip. Fiona had been distraught with anxiety that either her brother or Philip would be killed in another duel over the rumors. Harry had further annoyed her by insisting that Philip had been the source of the rumors and that Ted would teach him a lesson for bandying her name. She had lost all patience with Harry when he had tried to press his suit, saying she should marry him so that the rumors may be ended. At that point, she bid him a frosty goodbye and ensconced herself in her room. Ted had not returned by the time Fiona had gone to bed, and he was still asleep this morning, so she was reluctant to disturb him. She had no way of knowing what had transpired between him and Philip.

Restless, she gave up her attempt at embroidery and asked a footman to fetch her bonnet and shawl so she may take a walk in the garden while she waited on Ted to rise. Soon she was walking along the paths between the well-ordered flower beds. The garden at Red Oaks had always been a source of personal pride to her, as she had weeded and tended the flower beds frequently. But today, the state of her mind was such that she hardly noticed the beauty of her handiwork, nor did she hear the birdsong that usually brought a smile to her lips. Her mind lingered on her predicament.

She tried to imagine what may have happened when her brother had met with Philip. If their last meeting was any indication, only more violence could have followed. She hoped that they did not intend dueling again. But if Ted believed that Philip was behind the rumors, then that was exactly what would happen. She herself did not believe for a minute that Philip could have done something so base. After all his concern for her reputation while she was at his house, he could only be a true gentleman. In spite of what she had witnessed for herself at the Langton ball, part of her refused to accept that he was as bad as he was painted. After all, the same society that had dubbed him a villain had caused her present situation, and there was little enough substance to their accusations in the present situation. So why should they not have been mistaken in the past?

While pondering the dilemma, Fiona reached the rose garden, and there she sat down on a bench in the shade to think about what she could do to avert disaster. The garden was enchanting that morning, with sunlight playing on dappled leaves, and Fiona in her becoming, pale-green morning gown and bonnet trimmed with matching ribbon blended into the tableau. Surrounded by roses of every color, she looked like she had stepped into a work of art painted by Monet.

However, she was oblivious to all but her own internal turmoil and was startled when she heard a cough near her. Glancing up with a start, she saw the object of her thoughts standing in front of her as if she had conjured him up with sheer willpower. She stood up in confusion, and the jolt of joy she experienced at seeing him was short-lived as she tried to divine the reason for his unexpected presence. Had he come to set up another duel with her brother? Her mood swiftly turned into dismay and alarm as her anxiety increased severalfold, and she anticipated that her worst fears had been realized.

"Lord Sheffield," Fiona said once she had managed to calm herself and assume a composure that she did not feel. "What a surprise to see you here! Is it my brother you seek?"

"Miss Cavendish, I am here today to see you." Philip dived in, wanting to get it over with before he lost his nerve.

Fiona looked at him in surprise and relief that it wasn't Ted he sought and couldn't think of anything to say.

Philip made a stiff and formal bow and said, "Pray be seated, Miss Cavendish, for there is something I wish to speak to you about."

Too surprised to demur, Fiona sat without further comment.

"Miss Cavendish, the unfortunate consequences of our encounter have just reached my ears, and I truly regret the aspersions on your good name. I beg that you believe I had nothing to do with these vile rumors about you."

He paused here, and Fiona could do naught but gape at him with some semblance to a creature of the aquatic variety. Of the multitude of scenarios she had conjured prior to his unexpected arrival, this had not been one of those things. He had come not to discuss another duel but to deflect her brother's anger. Ted must not have seen him the previous day. Did Philip really believe that she blamed him for the rumors and had felt the need to apologize? Then she must disabuse him of that notion. He was as much a victim of the scandalmongers as she was. However, her heart fluttered a little that he had cared enough to come and see her, albeit with an unnecessary apology.

"Lord Sheffield, you need say no more. I do not hold you at all responsible for the unfortunate imaginings of others. And if there should be any blame, it lies with me. So please be at ease. Now, if you will please excuse me." She rose to her feet. Her anxiety was growing as her heart started to flutter in a rapid tattoo, and her mind jumped to the obvious conclusion that her worst fears were realized. Philip's statement that he had come to seek her out had not set her mind at rest. And if Ted saw him speaking to her, all hell would break loose. Her active imagination conjured up images of Ted killing Philip on the spot. The tragedy could still be averted if he left before her brother knew of his presence on their estate. So, thinking, she tried to cut short his obviously rehearsed speech.

His lordship looked startled at her abrupt dismissal and lost some of his schooled composure. In fact, one could even go so far as to say he looked distinctly embarrassed and uncomfortable.

"Please don't go, Miss Cavendish. That's not the only reason why I am here, I have something more to say," he said, speaking rapidly and reaching out a hand as if to stop her departure.

Intrigued, Fiona again seated herself and looked at him inquiringly. Could it be . . . ? Could he by some unexpected strokes of fortune have come to pay suit to her? Was it possible he reciprocated her feelings? These thoughts drew a rosy blush to her cheeks, and unable to meet his earnest eyes, she dropped her gaze to her hands that were loosely clasped on her lap.

Philip's next words interrupted her happy imaginings. "Miss Cavendish, in light of these unfortunate circumstances, I feel it is my duty to set things right."

At the mention of duty, her hopes faltered, even before they had fully formed. Her eyes shot up at him as a sudden glimmer of suspicion about his intentions occurred to her. Surprise and curiosity kept her silent, waiting for him to continue.

He appeared to take her silence as encouragement and continued, apparently oblivious to the effect his words were having on her. Her heart hammered against her chest so loudly that she was sure he would hear it. The phrase "be still my heart" now made sense to her, and she again looked away to hide her increasing blushes and emotional state. However, she wanted to see his expression; would they betray his feelings? When she took the courage to glance at him through lowered lashes, she was only disappointed to see that, instead of gazing at her with the admiration or adoration that she was used to seeing in her other suitors, he was playing with the signet ring on his right forefinger. She feared that anything she said would give away her own feelings.

Philip took a sidelong peep at her and continued. "You must agree that both our reputations have suffered . . . from recent events, and that there is only one solution that remains for us. We must marry at once. I know that we share no mutual affection for one another, but we must set our differences aside and agree that the situation calls for us to sacrifice our own feelings as a duty to preserve our family honor. Do not doubt that I hold you in the highest regard. If you will consent to be my lady, I will make it my mission to ensure that you are never unhappy."

His words extinguished all hope that he loved her, and for a moment, she felt disappointment, despair even. Then her valiant spirit rose to the occasion, and anger emerged and replaced her distress. Her eyes flashed with a militant gleam. Momentarily speechless as she tried to swallow the scalding words that were at the tip of her tongue, she seethed at the insult she felt he had handed her. Wherein she had expected pleas of undying devotion, he was offering her duty and family honor. He was willing to sacrifice himself for the sake of her and her family, was it? And he held her in highest regard! How dare him! She was not so woebegone as to accept offers of pity. She rose to her feet and drew herself up to her full height, which placed her just beneath his chiseled chin. Eyes flashing, she looked up at him, daring him to look away.

"My lord, while I am truly flattered by your concern, I must assure you that there is not the slightest need for you to immolate yourself at the altar of matrimony in my regard. I do not see any reason for us to wed. Even before this episode, I never had an ambition to wed at all, but knowing your disdain for the married state, I feel that I would rather die a spinster than marry you. Pray don't allow such trivialities as gossip to affect your life and take you from your chosen path of pleasure. I thank you for coming and bid you good day." Her dulcet tones dripped with ice that was intended to scald and freeze at the same time. Then, without waiting on his response, she turned on her heel and walked away from him.

"Miss Cavendish, Fiona, I beg you please reconsider." There was something in his voice, a desperation almost, a pitch she had never heard before, that made her pause for a moment as he continued. "I know that you have a poor opinion of me, but please believe that what I propose is in the best interest of everyone concerned. I can weather this storm by being a man, but surely even you can see that the damage to your own reputation cannot be ignored. Your life will be ruined."

She had heard enough. It was clear he did not love her, for he had not mentioned any affection at all. All he was offering was marriage of convenience. She looked at him sternly and spoke with a firmness that could brook no further argument. "Lord Sheffield, you have no need to worry about my life. I have enough relatives to do that. In fact, I have already received a proposal from a man who I know far better than I know you, and if I change my views on matrimony, I will consider accepting him as my husband. You may set your mind at ease." With a flash of skirts, she walked away from him.

CHAPTER TWENTY-FOUR

Walking rapidly toward the house in fury, Fiona's mind churned with conflicting emotions. Over the past few weeks, she had been reluctant to acknowledge even to herself the budding hopes taking root within her. Woven into those hopes had been the romantic notion that he would fall helplessly in love with her and entreat her to marry him. In her imagination, she had dreamed of marrying him and living happily thereafter. How harsh was reality and how different from her dreams! Seeing him lavish his attention on Lady Anne at the Langton ball had been torture to her poor, befuddled heart. She had seen the way he charmed that lady. However, even that instance had failed to erase all faith in her love from her tender breast. But, in the end, their encounter left no room for romance. He had dashed all her hopes and stomped the fragments of her dreams into the dirt with his words of honor and duty.

Despite her secret dreams, Philip's proposal had taken her by surprise. When she first recognized his intentions, sleeping butterflies had awakened and fluttered about fleetingly inside her, keeping rhythm to the rapid tattoo of her heart. She had waited with rapture to hear the words of love she longed for him to say. His proposal had squashed all her ardor, butterflies and all. There had been no mention of love or even the tiniest display of affection. He had not so much as looked at her or tried to hold her hand. Though marriage to him was her deepest desire, she could not permit herself to accept his proposal, knowing it came from pity and not affection. If and when she married, it would be for love, and since her heart was irrevocably given to him, she would remain unmarried for the rest of her life!

She had been so distraught that she could not recollect her exact response to him. Her pride had made her refuse his offer with some curtness and with no encouragement for him to ever offer again. Her mind was in such turmoil that she could barely see through the tears blinding her as she stumbled toward the house. How foolish she had been to expect him to profess his love or devotion. Philip Merton was a hardened rake and was hardly likely to love an unsophisticated maiden such as herself. His proposal had made that abundantly clear. It was merely a business proposition that was intended to rescue her from a life of solitude and censure that he was sure would result from her behavior. How *dare* he presume to think that she needed his charity or pity! He, who had no reputation to speak off, had dared to offer to help salvage hers. It was obvious he had felt obliged to offer. Of course, he had not meant it. Any suitor would have at the very least made the flowery speeches that every maiden expected from a prospective bridegroom. No! He had not meant it. It had merely been a grand gesture on his side made out of duty. Well, he could keep his precious gestures to himself. If she never saw him again, she would be immensely happy.

She entered the house almost at a run, seeking the sanctuary of her room. Once there, she flung herself onto her bed and sobbed to her heart's content until she could cry no more.

CHAPTER TWENTY-FIVE

Stunned by Fiona's abrupt refusal, Philip could only stare speechlessly after the haughtily held back of her departing figure, flabbergasted for a moment. He made no attempt to stop her. What was the point? She had made obvious her revulsion at his proposal. It was apparent that she held even the time spent in his company as abhorrent. He had made a mull of this. How could he have forgotten her opinion of him? Had he really thought that words of reason would win her over? Why had his polished speeches and renowned charm abandoned him when he needed them so direly? And the words of love he had rehearsed— why had he not been able to recall any of them? Why had he turned into a stiff, tongue-tied, bumbling fool in her presence?

He passed a hand over his eyes in dejection, and his shoulders slumped. How her eyes had flamed in derision, which he knew he deserved. He had failed miserably. All hope that she reciprocated some little amount of his feelings withered and died. He should have known that she wouldn't welcome a proposal from him. She would rather remain a spinster than wed him. She had said she would consider wedding another but not him. The thought of her wedding another was too painful to contemplate. His heart weighed like a ton of bricks, and a feeling of despondency descended over him like a storm cloud. He turned and swiftly walked to the stables where he had left his mount. Silently cursing himself for being such a fool, he mounted and spurred away to the nearest tavern to drown his sorrows.

Ted had intended to have a word with Fiona about Philip's intentions that morning, but his duty took precedence, and instead he had spent his day in riding about the home farm on the estate at Red Oaks and speaking to his tenant farmers, listening to their troubles and allaying their concerns. He was accompanied on this mission by both his bailiff, Hardley, and Bates. After a very tiring morning, they were taking cover from the sun by riding through some woods when a loud shot rang out at close quarters, making Bates's horse rear up in fear. The horse plunged about and nearly rammed into Ted. It was only through expert handling of the reins that Ted had been able to retain control of his own mount and remain seated on his saddle. Hardley was not quite such an expert rider, and his horse, Knobby, being a high-strung colt, bolted with his rider in the direction of the stables. After calming their respective mounts, Ted and Bates followed. By the time they reached the stables, Hardley had dismounted from his sweating steed and was standing, staring into the distance, mopping his forehead.

"You all right, Hardley?" Ted asked, dismounting and tossing his reins to a waiting groom.

"Yes, sir. It's just my steed took fright and carried me off."

"It was the damned shot. Bates, summon the gamekeeper. He should know better than to be shooting without warning."

"Beg your pardon, Sir Ted, but I think it wasn't the gamekeeper who should be blamed, but a poacher, more like."

"What's to do?" Harry Albrighton sauntered up to them and joined the conversation.

"Someone was shooting in the woods bordering the home farm and startled the horses," Ted explained, his annoyance mounting at this unexpected delay to his planned activities.

"Cousin! Who would do such a cork-brained thing?" Albrighton grimaced as if the very thought was distasteful.

"No one in their right senses. I have sent for Green, the gamekeeper, and we shall soon get to the bottom of this."

At that moment, the groom sent in search of Green came running back saying that Green was laid up with a touch of gout and was unable to attend Sir Cavendish just then.

"I'll be damned!" Albrighton swore loudly. "This is starting to smell of something unholy."

"Probably just a poacher, sir," Bates offered up again.

"This following your mishap with the carriage wheels, Cousin?" Albrighton interjected. "It's almost as if fate is contriving to lay you up, Ted."

"Don't know about fate and all," Hardley spoke up. "But I did see Lord Sheffield as I rode into the stables. His lordship looked mighty grim and was spurring his horse like a fury, he was."

Ted glanced at the groom, who confirmed that Sheffield had indeed been on the estate that morning.

"Cousin, that's too much of a coincidence, if you ask me." Albrighton sounded gleeful. "Given the bad blood between you and Sheffield, I'm just saying you should be more careful," he ended lamely, after Ted gave him a scorching look.

"I'll thank you to keep your conjectures to yourself, Cousin," Ted said awfully. "Philip Merton may be many things, but a coward he is not. If he wanted to shoot me, he would call me out and do it to my face, not scheme and shoot from hiding. Also, I see no need for Fiona to hear any of this."

"Of course, Cousin, there is no need to worry the poor chit. I will be the soul of discretion," Albrighton said ingratiatingly.

This only riled Ted up further, rather than reassuring him. He turned and marched into the house in search of his sister to determine the purpose of Philip's visit.

Resting in her room, trying to calm herself, Fiona was informed by a servant that Ted was awaiting her in the library. Composing herself, she went to meet her brother. Ted rose and came toward her as she rushed into the room. He immediately noticed that she was distraught and caught her by her arms.

"Fiona, dearest, whatever is wrong?" he exclaimed in alarm, all thought about the shot forgotten in that instant. "Is it the gossiping, old, nosy parkers, have they been troubling you?"

Fiona remained mute, tears streaming down her face. Ted led her to a sofa, gave her his kerchief, and held her until her sobs had quieted down. Then he rose to pour her a brandy and made her drink it. The drink stung the back of her throat, and Fiona choked and sputtered, but it also blazed a warm trail down her body and revived her. She pulled herself together and looked up at her brother.

"Feeling better, chickee?" he asked, smiling kindly at her.

Fiona nodded and smiled weakly back at him.

"Chick, there's something I must tell you. It's about Philip Merton."

"I too have something to tell you about him, but you are first. You did not challenge him to a duel again, did you?"

"Is that what's been worrying you? You can set your mind at rest on that account, because we have both agreed to bury the hatchet. I no longer bear him any ill will."

Fiona stared at her brother speechlessly, marveling at what could have caused this turn of events.

"In fact, he has proven that he is a gentleman by accepting his responsibility in this situation and has asked my permission to seek your hand in marriage, and I have granted it."

Fiona sprang to her feet in consternation. "So, he was here with your permission?"

"Has he been here already, then? What happened? Am I to wish you happy?"

"Oh, Ted! How could you?" Fiona cried indignantly.

"I thought you would be happy . . ." Ted stammered. "Do you think that I have not guessed how you feel about him? You have been not quite the thing since he left our house. You have sighed and moped for days on end. Now with all these dratted rumors, I thought it was time to let matters come to a head. That's why I gave Sheffield my blessing."

Fiona blushed a deep red but stood her ground. "My feelings have nothing to do with the matter, when he does not return them," she responded stonily. Much as she loved her brother, Fiona would have gladly broken a vase over his head at that moment.

"Why? Did he not propose, then?" Ted was puzzled.

"He did ask for my hand in marriage, if that's what you call a proposal. A man might approach a cup of poison with more enthusiasm than he showed to the idea of marrying me. I turned him down, of course."

"What an idiot!" Ted muttered, and Fiona looked at him in outrage.

"Not you, dearest. Him! I should have known that he would make a mull of things."

Fiona stared at him uncomprehendingly. Ted shook his head.

"Oh, little one! Don't you get it? He is in love with you but refuses to acknowledge it even to himself for fear of being hurt. Love has not been kind to him, and he runs shy of being burned again."

"Ted, what are you saying? You are not making any sense. How do you know any of this?"

Ted patted his sister's hand comfortingly while he related what had transpired during his interview with Philip. As he spoke, he noticed his sister first listening entranced and then becoming increasingly distraught until tears appeared in her eyes and trickled unhindered down her cheeks.

"Oh dear! The poor man! It is no wonder he has lost faith in love," she declared, wiping her tears and sniffing when Ted finally concluded his narrative.

"But you can change that, can't you? He has fallen in love with you, chick," Ted said impatiently.

"How do you know that? Did he say as much to you?" Fiona asked, eagerness creeping into her voice. "If he cared about me so much, he would not have flirted so shamelessly with that floozy."

"Don't be a goose, Fiona. Lady Anne is not a floozy but an independent spirit, much as yourself. And just like you, she has been maligned by a society which cannot abide a woman who can think for herself. She and Philip are friends and nothing more. As anyone with some sense will know. As for Philip declaring his feelings for you, no British man in his right senses would do such a thing! But even a blind man who spent any time in both of your company would be able to discern your feelings for each other. And I'm not blind."

Fiona stared at him in dismay, and tears rose afresh to her eyes.

Ted patted her shoulder affectionately. "Now don't despair, chickee. It's not as bad as all that. Give it some time, and he will come to understand his own heart and will be back to pursue you as a proper suitor. I know the stubborn fool well. When Philip wants something, he will not give up that easily. The last time he was in love, I lost out to him. Do not give up on him, love."

This statement only served to make Fiona sob more loudly. "Ted, you don't understand, he thinks I am going to marry Harry," she cried.

THE HOYDEN AND THE RAKE

"What!" Ted roared. "Now where would he get such a birdbrained idea?"

"I told him so, in anger," Fiona wailed.

"Oh God! What a bumble broth this is. Are you seriously considering wedding Harry? That fellow does not have two farthings to rub together and is after your fortune, as you must realize."

"I know, and I have no least inclination to wed Cousin Harry, but when Philip said that he only wanted to marry me to rescue me from scandal and save my reputation, I told him that I did not need rescuing as Harry had already offered." Fiona covered her face in her hands at the memory of her own foolish behavior.

"Now don't get yourself into a pucker, chick. I'll talk to old Phil and sort this mess out. Just give me a few days, and you will see that it will all work out just the way it should."

Brother and sister were so wrapped up in their own conversation that they did not notice the window had been open. Nor did they notice that their conversation had not been as private as they thought. It had been heard by another pair of ears whose owner did not like the description of being "pockets to let." A shadowy figure who slunk away at this point. Once a safe distance away from earshot, he let fall some choice cuss words, leaving no doubt of his feelings about "high in the instep misses," "high-handed relatives," and "interfering nobility."

CHAPTER TWENTY-SIX

Fiona spent a restless night and woke up at dawn. Yearning to be outside, she donned her habit and went down for an early ride. She had her horse saddled and—craving solitude—refused the company of a groom and rode out. Galloping, she reached her usual spot in the meadow, where she dismounted and let her horse free to graze while she sat against a tree and watched the sunrise. Her mind invariably wandered to the beloved man who had dominated her thoughts since her conversation with Ted. Why could the infernal man not have spoken his feelings instead of talking about "the regard" he held her in? Regard indeed! Fiddlesticks!

Her mind went back to the few moments where had let his guard down while she had been his unexpected guest, and she smiled to herself. How pleasant those moments spent in his company had been. What a fool she had been to dismiss the opportunity to spend a lifetime with him so hastily, in pride. Ted may well believe that Philip would offer again, but she now clearly recalled how wounded and hurt he had looked when she had cursorily refused his proposal. His shoulders had slumped in abject dejection. He had avoided love and marriage for years to avoid being hurt, and she had succeeded in hurting him. Her mood turned despondent as she pursued this negative train of thought. Perhaps she should seek him out and apologize yet again? This time for her rudeness. Would he forgive her? Surely if he loved her as Ted claimed, he might give her another chance to redeem herself. Oh! Why, why must she always show herself in such a poor light when he was around?

Her thoughts were interrupted by hoofbeats, and seeing a lone horseman in black riding up, her heart quickened. Could it be him? As he approached closer, she was disappointed to recognize Harry Albrighton. Annoyed that her solitude had been interrupted, she hoped he wouldn't linger. Albrighton dismounted and came and stood by her without waiting for an invitation.

"I see that you are out early, Coz," he began. "Just as well, for I have something to ask you."

Guessing what was coming, she forestalled him by saying, "I am sorry, Harry, but my mind has not changed since yesterday."

"I am sorry to hear that, Fiona. May I inquire whether there is another man in the picture?"

Hoping to warn him off once for all, Fiona jumped on the excuse and said truthfully, "Alas, Cousin Harry, you are very astute and have guessed my secret. Indeed, I have given my heart to another."

"And are your affections returned?" Albrighton asked.

"I believe they may be." Crossing her fingers behind her, Fiona prayed that her words should be true.

"In that case, you force my hand and leave me no recourse. Please forgive me, Cousin." Saying this, Albrighton grabbed Fiona with one hand and pressed a square of damp fabric against her face with the other.

Too surprised to protest, Fiona smelled a sickly-sweet odor permeate her nose. The last words she heard as she blacked out were "Gretna Green."

Albrighton lifted her onto his horse and led it a short way to the lane where his curricle was parked. There he transferred the unconscious girl into the vehicle and, leaving the horse loose, climbed on himself and drove off.

Philip had not had a peaceful repose either. He ruminated over his meeting with Fiona and spent the night interspersed with self-recrimination at the way he had proposed to her. After the first shock of her abrupt refusal had worn off, his common sense took over. Setting aside his wounded feelings, he analyzed the whole situation with an unbiased outlook. Being a man of superior intelligence, it did not take him long to discern where he had erred. Her skittish behavior and attempts to dismiss him, which he had perceived as aversion to his presence, were hardly surprising in retrospect. The rumors and the duel had both contrived to make them an object of gossip, and she was right in trying to avoid further scandal. And he himself had not helped the situation in any measure. Why had he not recognized her emotional state and reassured her? His silver tongue had deserted him, and he had been as wooden and tongue-tied as a schoolboy. It was no wonder that she had turned him down. What had happened to all his rehearsed speeches and words of admiration? Why had he forgotten them all? The circumstances of their last encounter at the Langton ball and his own stellar performance with Lady Anne's aid had probably cemented her impression of him as a rake.

These thoughts kept Philip awake in his bed, tossing and turning and groaning aloud at his own stupidity, until finally, at dawn, he rose bleary-eyed but with a determination. He would go to her again, and this time he would do it properly. He would speak from his heart, and she would see his sincerity and surely change her mind. It no doubt made his task more difficult knowing that she held him in such poor regard. However, he would drop to bended knee and hold her until she agreed to marry him. For the very thought of her marrying another was unbearable. And she might well agree to marriage with Albrighton just to gain her inheritance. For who could blame her for wanting to be independent? Lashing her to that snively weasel was not to be tolerated.

Philip yelped as the thought of Fiona wedding Albrighton had made him wield his razor with unwonted force and nick himself in the jaw. As he completed the rest of his toilette with Samuels's assistance, he formed a plan of action. He would approach Ted Cavendish and ask him to intercede with Fiona to make her see reason. He would confess that he had made a big mess of the marriage proposal and ask Ted for help. If he could get Ted to speak on his behalf, she may be inclined to give him a second chance. With this in mind, he had his horse, Tempest, saddled and rode out to Red Oaks. There, he found Ted seated at breakfast and was invited to join his host.

"What brings you here this early, Sheffield?" Ted asked, forking a mouthful of eggs. Philip sat down, gratefully accepting the steaming coffee that Sudbury poured for him.

It wasn't until the butler had left them alone that he replied. "I am afraid I made a mull of the business, Ted. Your sister has taken me in dislike and refused me offhand."

"It doesn't surprise me, you clod pole, your notions of love are enough to send any sensible female running away screaming."

"What is to be done, then?" Philip asked in despondent tones.

"Give her some time to cool off. I don't doubt that she will be more receptive if you couch your proposal in terms of affection, rather than as if you were negotiating the purchase of horseflesh at Tattersalls."

Philip scowled at this well-aimed set down and focused his attention on rearranging the food on his plate in gloomy silence. It was at this moment that Sudbury entered again, accompanied by a groom from Ted's estate. The groom, who looked very agitated, approached Cavendish to whisper in his ear. The effect of his words on Cavendish was remarkable. He turned white and shot up with a curse, sending his chair toppling backward.

Raising an eyebrow in surprise, Philip rose also. "Is anything amiss, Ted?" he inquired.

"It's Fiona," Ted barked out, not pausing as he left the room in haste. "I am sorry, I must leave you, Sheffield, for my sister hasn't returned from her morning ride. She left almost three hours ago, and her horse has just now returned without her."

Philip blanched on hearing this. Fiona was missing. What could have befallen her? His mind promptly conjured up the worst possible reasons, including grave injury and even death. His heart accelerated and plummeted at the same time, making his chest feel icy cold as fear crept within him. He hurried to keep up with Ted, asking a barrage of questions in hushed and anxious tones.

"She cannot have gone far? Surely a skilled rider like her would not have come to any harm, Cavendish?" he said, trying to believe his own words.

Ted kept walking without a response, and his silence only compounded Philip's fears for Fiona's well-being. As they entered the stables together, they were met by a flurry of activity, and one of the grooms came running to meet them. Ted addressed the man, who looked very worried.

"Thimble, ready my racing curricle posthaste."

Thimble cast his eyes down and twisted his hat in his hands, revealing his worry. "M'lord, Master Albrighton drove out a while back, after Miss Fiona had left this morning," he imparted, looking crestfallen to be the bearer of more bad news.

Ted stopped short. "Albrighton? Now, that is mighty peculiar! Where could he have gone?"

"I would not mention it, m'lord, save that he took your racing curricle."

Ted cursed long and loud at this.

A nasty suspicion began to form in Philip's mind. One that aroused such a flash of insane jealousy and pain in his breast that it surprised him. "Fiona mentioned that Albrighton had offered for her. Is it possible that they eloped together?" he inquired in a dangerously quiet voice.

"Never! Albrighton has been dangling after her this age and more, but she has not paid him the slightest attention. Truth be told, it was to escape from being forced into a betrothal with him in my absence that she ran away that time when you were obliged to rescue her."

Philip swore profusely. "Damnation! Ted, I have never been able to fathom how you put up with him, heir or not. He is one slippery customer!"

"That's neither here nor there. The real question is why are they both missing at the same time? This reeks of something rotten." Ted's brow furrowed as he tried to solve the mystery.

"Perhaps they are not together. She may have turned him down again last evening, and he may have left in a huff. She could have ridden out this morning and been thrown and is perhaps now lying somewhere hurt!" Just voicing his fears made Philip feel his apprehension increase, and despair momentarily made him weak-limbed.

His words spurred Ted into action. He shouted out orders that all the stable hands and grooms were to form a search party and then gave instructions that the entire estate and countryside should be scoured.

He turned to Sheffield and asked, "Are you going with us, Phil?"

Philip shook his head. "I will ride Tempest and make inquiries in the village and then along the highway to see if anyone has seen Albrighton's vehicle." So saying, he mounted his waiting horse, and without waiting for the search party to leave, set off at a gallop in the direction of the village.

On reaching the village general store, he gave the reins of his horse to a small boy who ran up eagerly. He made inquiries of various people, but no one had seen a "flash" curricle go through. Disappointed, he was about to turn back when a small hand tugged on his sleeve. Looking down, he saw the grubby face of the little boy who had been watching his horse. Thinking that he was wanting to be paid, Philip reached in his purse for a coin, but the boy pulled on his sleeve again.

"Be ye looking for Miss Cavendish?" the boy asked.

Philip looked at him in surprise. "Yes. Have you seen her today?" he asked eagerly.

The boy nodded. "I saw one of them racing things go past just after dawn. The gent was in a mighty hurry and did not slow down, and I had to jump out of the way or be run over. But when they sped past I see'd Miss Cavendish in there sitting alongside the gent, and she looked like she be sleepin'," he imparted.

"Which way did they go?" Philip barked, taking the reins from him and jumping on his horse.

"North, sir."

"North!" His suspicions confirmed, Philip swore lustily. Then they were on their way to Gretna Green.

"Young man, you have been of great service." He tossed the lad a coin. "There is another for you if you carry a message to Sir Ted Cavendish that I am going north after his sister and that he should follow immediately. Run as quickly as you can."

The boy set off at a brisk pace. Philip mounted his horse and turned northward. He was convinced now that Fiona had been deceived by Albrighton to accompany him to Gretna Green with a hasty marriage in mind. What had Albrighton used to wield her to his will? Had she been forced or harmed? The very thought of Fiona in the hands of a slimy, spineless dandy such as Albrighton made Philip see red. That poor girl should not be forced to marry one such as Albrighton. He would stop them at all costs. They had over two hours of lead on him, so he had to make haste if he wanted to intercept them before they reached Gretna Green, the destination for elopements.

He hoped that Cavendish would follow posthaste with reinforcements, for Albrighton may refuse to let her go, and it could turn ugly. His thoughts made him spur his horse onward, but Tempest needing no further urging ran like the wind.

The countryside flashed past in a blur as man and horse rode on a mission. Time flew by, and he rode without stopping for food or water, but he knew that Tempest was tiring and that he would have to stop soon and change horses. It was late afternoon when he glimpsed the curricle ahead of him. The sight made him encourage Tempest anew.

Albrighton must have spotted his pursuer, for he whipped his team harder, and the curricle lurched forward. But they were no match for Tempest. His master's anxiety communicated itself to the horse, and the great beast sprang forth in a final burst of energy, and Sheffield drew abreast of the curricle. He saw Fiona hanging on to the seat of the curricle, tears of relief and fear glistening in her eyes as she cried to Albrighton to stop. Albrighton whipped his horses more, and when Philip made to reach for his reins, he flicked his whip at Tempest. Tempest, having been named for his wild temper, took offense at this and reared up, and Philip was hard-pressed to keep his seat. The much-tried horses pulling the curricle panicked, and they reared up in a frenzy and went haywire. Albrighton lost the reins to hold on to the seat, and the curricle went off the road. The speed they were going made it inevitable that the curricle should overturn. Both Fiona and Albrighton were thrown clear and were lucky to land on some bushes.

Alighting in haste, Philip ran around the fallen curricle toward the pair to ascertain if they had been injured, only to find himself facing the deadly end of a pistol held by Albrighton, who also held a struggling Fiona against him with his arm around her.

"Stay where you are, Sheffield, or I'll blow out your brains," he called.

Philip held up his hands and speaking in a controlled voice said, "Let her go, Albrighton, it's over."

"It's over for you, Sheffield. I should have put a period to you long since for your interference in my affairs."

"What drivel is this? As far as I know, you and I have never crossed paths."

"You were too high and mighty to acknowledge me in those days, but not so your beloved Elizabeth. I loved her long before you came along, but she chose you for your wealth and title. She may have wedded you, but she never loved you. She tired of you and your country ways, and when she returned to town, she turned to me again. Did you know that I was her lover, and she was going to leave you to be with me? Except I wanted your fortune too, so I asked her to kill you. She resisted until I got her with child. Fate dealt me a nasty hand when you survived the pistol shot, but she was killed by her fall." Albrighton paused, savoring his enemy's dismay at his revelations.

"This time it will be different. I will marry Fiona and control her fortune, and you will die a very painful death right here for interfering in my plans twice."

"No." His mind reeling from these disclosures, Philip strove to maintain his calm demeanor. "You are forgetting Ted. He will never accept this marriage, and as Fiona does not stand to inherit until her majority, you will be pockets to let," he said, trying to gain time as his mind scrambled to find a way to secure Fiona's safety.

"Ah! Cavendish! Another thorn in my side. I had hoped he would meet his end fighting in the continent, or that Fiona would wed me in his absence, but I was thwarted there again. Ted will join you soon enough in the afterlife, never fear. I do not much care for the measly allowance he makes me, it really does cramp my style. I would much rather have all his estates, as well as his sister's fortune. I have engaged a hardened highwayman to take care of good old Ted, but thus far Ted has had a charmed existence and managed to escape death. But his luck won't last forever. Trust me, Sheffield, Ted's days on this earth are numbered. And once he is gone, Fiona will be much more amenable as a wife and produce me an heir and a spare. Then, if she were to come to an untimely death, well, who can blame me?" He let out a roar of laughter at his own cunningly crafted, evil plan.

Fiona, who had listened to this recounting in mounting horror, screamed out, "No! Please don't harm Ted! I will talk to him, he will keep you in funds until I come into my majority. Please don't kill him. I beg you. I will do as you wish and marry you. Please spare his life."

"Perhaps I will when my dear wife beseeches me so sweetly. If your brother listens to reason, he has nothing to fear. Do not even think about divulging my schemes to him, my sweet, for you will soon be wedded to me, and we will spend this night together as man and wife to consummate our marriage. And you will be an obedient and dutiful wife ever after if you wish to save your brother's life. What's more, by law you cannot bear witness against your own dear husband. As for this self-righteous rake, he has but moments to live, so you had best say your goodbyes." Albrighton laughed.

Fiona clung to Albrighton, crying, "Let him go, Harry. Why should you dirty your hands with his death? He means nothing to me. Let us not start our life with his death on our conscience."

"Sheffield deserves what's coming to him, and even you, my dear coz, can't prevent it," Albrighton said with a sinister chuckle.

"If your grief is with me, you can have your revenge on me, but I beg you please let her go." Philip sought desperately to find a way out of this mess by appealing to his adversary's good sense. "If you run away with her, Cavendish may well disown her, and you will be saddled with an unwilling wife. You may not get her fortune."

"Developed a tendre for my cousin have you, poor sod? What an unexpected bonus! It is indeed poetic justice that I end up with the girl you love now, just as you married my lover. Don't you worry about my prospects, my dearest Fiona will become independently wealthy as soon as she reaches her majority. And once we are wed at Gretna, Cavendish would never allow his dear sister to be ill-used. So he will fork up the blunt to keep me in good stead as well. After all, I will be his brother-in-law as well as his heir. Your prospects, on the other hand, are rather bleak. I think I will shoot you in the stomach. I've heard that the agony is excruciating, and it will be a while before you die. It's a pity that we can't stay to watch, but Gretna Green awaits us." He matched his actions to his words and pointed the gun at Philip's middle.

On hearing this fiendish plot, Philip paled perceptibly but was amazed to see the fury with which Fiona screamed and kicked against her abductor, and after a tremendous struggle, she managed to wrench herself from his grasp. But instead of running to safety, the intrepid girl positioned herself in front of the pistol just as Albrighton's finger tightened on the trigger, preventing him from pulling it. He cursed loudly and pushed her away and flung her from him with such force that she went flying against the overturned curricle. Her head connected with the wheel, and she lay still.

Her timely action had given Philip his chance, and he now sprang on Albrighton and tried to wrest the gun from him. Albrighton struggled and held fast. He dealt Philip a blow to the jaw, but Philip held on tenaciously to the hand holding the pistol. Albrighton tried to point the pistol at Philip just as Philip tried to tug it away. In the ensuing struggle there was a loud retort, and the pistol went off.

Philip felt a sharp pain on his left side, and for a minute still held on to the smoking pistol in his adversary's hand, then he slowly sank to the ground. Just then, the sound of hoofbeats in the distance signaled an approaching carriage. With a look of hatred at the fallen man, Albrighton ran and unharnessed one of the horses from the curricle and, jumping on, took off in haste.

Philip lay on the ground, motionless for a moment as blackness threatened to envelop him. The thought that Fiona had sustained injury imbued him with the strength to fight to remain conscious. Holding his hand against the injury to his side, he tried to crawl toward her. She only lay a few paces away, but it seemed like a mile as his vision blurred with the effort. His progress was awfully slow and painful, and he was soaked in sweat and blood by the time he finally reached her side. He rested his back against the curricle and pulled her close, and holding her in his arms, peered anxiously into her face. Checking her throat for a pulse, he threw up a prayer of thanks when he found one. She had a small cut on her forehead where she had hit her head, and it had bled. The sight of the blood on her beloved face created untold havoc in his mind. He called out to her repeatedly, but she did not respond.

"My darling girl! My love! Please open your eyes," he cried frantically over and over again, but she lay still. He covered her face with kisses while beseeching her with every endearment in his considerable vocabulary, yet she showed no signs of movement. The pain from his wound was eclipsed by the agony caused by the thought of losing her. She had so bravely risked her life and put herself in front of the pistol only to save his worthless life. If only he could revive her. He would have given his life for a drop of water with which to dampen her forehead or moisten her lips, for surely that would revive her. But there was no water to be had at hand. He held her closer, his eyes misting with tears as he pressed kisses over her face, imploring her to come back to him until he grew hoarse with despair.

Thus it was that when Fiona aroused from her faint moments later, she found herself clasped in the arms of her beloved and being showered with kisses. She can be forgiven for wanting to dwell at that moment for a spell. She listened with ardor as she heard him speak all the words of love she had yearned for in no uncertain terms, and it filled her heart with gladness. His adoring words were everything she had desired and thought impossible. Therefore, she cannot be faulted for staying still and delighting in the situation a little longer. At last, her eyes fluttered open, and she peeped at him. She was moved by the anguish in his distraught face, and she looked up at him wonderingly. Was this the same man who everyone described as heartless? She put up a hand to wipe his tears, and he caught it in his and kissed it. They stayed that way for a delicious interlude, their eyes conveying what their hearts were feeling more eloquently than words ever could. Then she saw the blood on his coat and sat up with a cry.

"You are hurt," she said. "And here I am lying down instead of tending to you."

"It's a mere scratch," he replied, reluctant to let her go.

"Nevertheless, 'tis bleeding profusely and must be attended to."

Standing briskly, she pulled up her dress and started ripping her petticoat to use as a bandage, and seeing him watching her with amusement, she ordered him to remove his coat and shirt.

He jestingly complained that she was constantly trying to see him in undress, but he endeavored to please. But this proved difficult with his injury, and she was obliged to gently help him out of his coat. Then asking him to lie still, she deftly opened his shirt to get at his wound. She was relieved to see that the bullet had not entered his chest but had cut through his side below the ribs. It was a shallow wound, but as is the nature of such wounds, was bleeding profusely. She offered up a prayer that he had so narrowly missed being killed. Fashioning strips of her petticoat into a pad, she used others to bind the wound up tightly. The whole procedure was very painful and caused Philip to break into a sweat, though he bore it manfully without a sound. He watched her with adoring eyes, and when she tightened the knot, he quietly fainted.

She sat down beside him on the road, and pulling his head onto her lap, held him to her bosom, waiting for rescue to arrive. She did not have long to wait, for the noise of the approaching carriage grew ever nearer, and soon her brother's coach drew up next to them. Ted jumped out even before the coach came to a stop and was taken aback by the dramatic tableau that met his eyes.

CHAPTER TWENTY-SEVEN

O nce more, Philip gained consciousness in the guest chamber at Red Oaks. It was with a sense of déjà vu that he again thought there was an angel seated by the fireside. Hearing him move, his angel rose and approached him, gazing at him with such adoration that he could only grin at her while thanking the heavens for this precious gift bestowed on his unworthy self.

"You really must stop coming into gentlemen's chambers when they are not dressed. It is becoming an unbelievably bad habit," he quipped.

"Alas, once again I find that I must thank you for rescuing me," she said demurely and leaned down as if to kiss his cheek but instead whispered teasingly against his ear. "I'll have you know that I have stayed in this particular gentleman's chamber all night."

An arm of surprising strength, for an injured man, shot up and pulled her down and held her. Fiona was so thoroughly kissed that she felt breathless and weak. Laughing, she broke away, and summoning her most stern demeanor, she said, "I'll have you know, sir, that my brother will take umbrage at your behaving thus with his lady sister."

"I will inform your brother that he has thus far been very remiss and neglected your upbringing. He should not encourage you to wander around the countryside, undressing strange men and creeping into their bedchambers at all hours of the day. Your lack of maidenly modesty in hoisting up your skirts to rip your petticoat in full view of a notorious rake does need a special mention as well. He needs to handle you with a firmer hand."

"And what if my brother should disagree with you?" she prompted, stepping closer.

"Why then, I will have no recourse but to take your instruction upon myself without further ado." He pulled her back onto him and claimed her lips again.

After a brief and delightful interlude, he asked what had happened to Albrighton.

"Our villainous cousin has escaped and is probably on his way to France. Ted is talking to his foreign office connections in Paris to see if they can locate him. He is determined to bring him to justice and clear the blot on our family honor. He is appealing to the crown to remove Harry from the line of succession as well. Cousin Sadie is awfully distraught, and she kept beseeching Ted on her son's behalf until Ted tired and packed her off to Bath. So, at least I have finally escaped her reign of terror," she said, running her delicate fingertips over the lines of his face. Philip captured her fingers to kiss them one by one as she continued.

"You are being hailed as the hero of the hour for your brave rescue of an innocent and frail maiden from a terrible fate."

"'Innocent and frail'? I know of no such maiden." Philip hid his smile and inspected her thumb before kissing it tenderly.

His remark earned him a tweak of his nose as she freed her hand from his grasp and sprang up.

"Would you treat a poor, wounded man so unkindly? Heartless hoyden!" he cried, reaching out his hand in a pitiful way, his eyes sparkling with mirth that belied his woebegone expression.

"You, my lord, are no longer to be pitied, as the fickle members of the ton have condescended to forgive your dubious past and are willing to accept you back with open arms," Fiona said, sitting down primly on the edge of the bed. "All the mamas are already lining up their daughters to drop their kerchiefs for you. You will have your bevy of beauties and debutantes."

"God forbid! I couldn't face the prospect of having green debutantes thrust at me from all directions."

"You prefer blonde widows, I take it?" she demanded playfully.

Philip's expression turned serious. "Anne is an old and dear friend, and we were only playacting that night to make you change your mind about me."

"I know that you silly man, I am only teasing. Anne has been to visit with me, and we have become good friends. We find we have much in common in terms of independent thoughts. Anne has offered to be a sponsor once I set up the school to help girls from poor straits."

"I am glad of that, for she will be as good a friend to you as she has been to me." Philip's eyes glowed with tenderness as he reached again for her hand.

Fiona gave him a coy glance beneath demurely lowered eyelashes. "Lady Anne has asked me to sit for a portrait in the gardens at Red Oaks. She mentioned that it may be a gift to a great friend. Do you know aught about this?" Fiona asked, all innocence while mischief danced in her green eyes.

Philip colored but held her eyes. "Lady Anne knows me well, and she saw through all my excuses to stay away from you. Once she understood the situation, she gave me a great lecture for high-handedly deciding that you were better off without me. She said that it was your decision to make and not mine. It was she who encouraged me to come and ask for your hand. You know the rest."

Fiona's cheeks gained a pink hue, and she had the grace to look abashed.

"Philip, I . . ." She started trying to apologize, but Philip squeezed her hand and forestalled her from finishing.

"Fiona, please allow me to say what I should have said when I made that foolish proposal. My dearest girl, ever since you wandered into my life, you have ignited warring flames in my withered heart, bringing it to life. I feared that my past put you out of my reach, and I tried to deny my feelings. When you rejected my proposal, it was one of the worst moments of my miserable life, for all hope was lost. When I thought that you had been taken by that scoundrel, my only fear was for your safety. If you were spared, I would gladly have died unloved. But what must you do, you intrepid girl, but throw yourself so bravely—and might I add foolishly—in front of that pistol to save my wretched life? It was then that I dared hope that you returned my affections. Uninvited, you crept into my home and heart, and I now wish to hold you there and cherish you until I breathe my last breath. So, my dear girl, will you put me out of my misery and say you will marry me?"

Philip's eyes were very tender as he spoke, and Fiona gazed into them, her face aglow with happiness. Her saucy smile made her look endearing as with a dimple deepening next to her mouth she said, "You took your time, my dearest rake. I knew I loved you from the very first moment when you called me a hoyden."

If he had any further doubt, it was dispelled when she threw her arms around him and kissed him with every ounce of passion her tiny frame could muster.

The End

ABOUT THE AUTHOR

Victoria Price is the pen name of an author of Indian origin living in the US. She is an avid fan of romance, especially historical novels, and has published other literary novels and children's books.

For more information about the author, please visit www.vpriceauthor.com.

Made in the USA
Monee, IL
29 June 2024

60932970R00100

CPSIA information can be obtained
at www.ICGtesting.com
Printed in the USA
LVHW03s2312060718
582846LV00003B/4/P